A Candlelight Ecstasy Romance ®

"WHAT ARE YOU MADE OF, STEEL?" GAR'S EYES NARROWED ON HER, SEARING HER WITH THE HEAT OF HIS GLANCE.

"How can you turn on and off just like that? Or is making love just a game to you?"

"Are you telling me that you love me?" Jessica questioned, her voice raised in disbelief.

"I'm saying that I'd love to make love to you." Gar corrected her, as if talking to a slow child. "Come off it; you've been around long enough to know that I want you."

"Funny, my age is supposed to grant me wisdom, but I don't have the wisdom to cope with you. And now I'm suddenly glad I don't. This is one little fish you'll have to chalk up as getting away. Don't worry, there are plenty more out there in the ocean who are ready to be hooked and would be more than happy to warm your bed. But I won't," she promised. . . .

CANDLELIGHT ECSTASY ROMANCES ®

ONLY FOR LOVE

Tira Lacy

A CANDLELIGHT ECSTASY ROMANCE ®

Published by
Dell Publishing Co., Inc.
1 Dag Hammarskjold Plaza
New York, New York 10017

Dell ® TM 681510, Dell Publishing Co., Inc.
Candlelight Ecstasy Romance®, 1,203,540, is a registered trademark of Dell Publishing Co., Inc.,
New York, New York.

ISBN: 0–440–16676–4

Printed in the United States of America
First printing—March 1984

For Marissa, my daughter, and Susanna, her friend. You both have so many things ahead for you. I wish you all of them . . . one at a time!

To Our Readers:

We have been delighted with your enthusiastic response to Candlelight Ecstasy Romances®, and we thank you for the interest you have shown in this exciting series.

In the upcoming months we will continue to present the distinctive sensuous love stories you have come to expect only from Ecstasy. We look forward to bringing you many more books from your favorite authors and also the very finest work from new authors of contemporary romantic fiction.

As always, we are striving to present the unique, absorbing love stories that you enjoy most—books that are more than ordinary romance.

Your suggestions and comments are always welcome. Please write to us at the address below.

Sincerely,

The Editors
Candlelight Romances
1 Dag Hammarskjold Plaza
New York, New York 10017

CHAPTER ONE

". . . and a boyfriend will come into your life, one who has loads of good looks and lots of money." Sheila, Jessica's best friend and neighbor, took a another sip from her wine goblet, her knowing eyes full of mischief as she peered over the large crystal bowl of her glass.

"Not on a bet!" Jessica stated emphatically, watching as Sheila laid the cards on the plushly carpeted floor. "I'm perfectly capable of fending for myself. I make an excellent living with my dress shop and the etiquette classes are fun and gravy money for me. What in heaven's name would I need a man for? Shuffle those cards, Sheila, and begin again."

Sheila raised a plump, beringed hand to her forehead, closing her eyes as if in meditation.

"The cards know. Destiny cannot be altered by anyone but you. Choose your path well and walk down it carefully, for there will be drastic changes in the near future," she intoned in a deep voice before opening her eyes. "If you live well and true, there will be a pocket full of rainbows waiting for you." She gave a breezy wink that made Jessica laugh despite herself.

"Mom, can Susanna and I go down to the grocery store for some more soft drinks? A few of the kids might drop in tonight." A dark-auburn–haired teenager stood at the entrance to the kitchen, obviously impatient to be on her way. Jessica glanced up, surprised as always to see just how lovely her fifteen-year-old was. She had bloomed in the past two years, picking up her father's coloring and features while keeping the natural grace of her mother. Tight jeans encased a neatly packaged figure, with a blue and white striped jersey top accenting the girl's small shoulders and long supple neck. *Ah, youth,* Jessica thought with a sigh.

"Sure, there are a few dollars in the sugar bowl. But take some eye shadow off first, honey. Remember, a light touch, not a heavy hand, Marissa," Jessica admonished with a smile. Marissa made a grimace but went to the small kitchen mirror and dabbed at the offending eye shadow with a soft Kleenex.

"Has anyone told you how lucky you are?" Sheila said under her breath as they watched

Marissa carrying out her mother's instructions. "Not only is she beautiful, charming, and full of fun, but she listens to you."

Jessica chuckled, her eyes still on her daughter. "Yes, I know. Only don't make too big a thing out of it. There've been plenty of blow-ups around here."

"Yes, but not like the ones around my house! Not even the dogs listen to me!"

"My God, how would you know? With five dogs and four boys you're always getting their names confused! I've yet to hear you call the children or the dogs by their right names!" Jessica laughed aloud.

As she looked across the table at her best friend, Sheila was about to say something about how lovely Jessica was, but she remembered just how much it had stilted the conversation the last time, and bit her tongue.

"That's only fair. They call me 'man' instead of Mom half the time!" Sheila retorted. "I think they need a lesson in sex education, but that's their father's job. I wouldn't know where to begin telling the boys about the birds and the bees."

"You haven't told them yet?"

"No, I figure they can find out the same way Jack and I did—on the streets. That's half the fun."

Marissa walked back through the room on her way out the door. A grin showed her small dimples. "Maybe I should send Mom to your house, Mrs. Hamilton. She not only thoroughly explains the birds and the bees, but she also gives a clinical observation on unbalanced hormones and winds up with a running commentary on sex and its evils. By the time she finishes with them, the boys will think twice about even considering marriage," the young girl teased.

"In that case, keep her away from my door, will you, Marissa? I'm looking forward to each of them leaving my home for one of their own as soon as possible. I'd hate to see dirty socks and underwear in my future for the rest of my life."

Marissa giggled, waved, and was out the door.

Sheila sighed, taking another sip of cool white wine. "Honestly, Jessica, I wish the boys would latch on to Marissa and follow her example. She's an absolute doll!"

"Thanks for the compliment, but I'd prefer that Marissa stay footloose and fancy-free for a few more years yet. She'll have plenty of time later, when she's finished college and knows more about life," Jessica said dryly.

Her friend's eyes got a curious light. "You really don't care much for men, do you? I've only seen you date maybe five times in the past year, and then only because the men were so persistent." She hesitated a moment. "Are you sure you aren't bitter?"

"Bitter? No. Wary? Yes. These days everyone

is into swinging sex and one-night stands. That's just not enough for me. I like the old-fashioned things: home, children, a man who enters the door at six and doesn't leave at nine."

Sheila's eyes opened wide. She'd never gotten Jessica to discuss men before. This was a whole new side to her fairly reserved friend.

"And what's wrong with an occasional one-night stand? It's happened to the best of 'em and it sure beats loneliness sometimes."

Jessica lounged back against the cushion of the chair. "Nothing beats loneliness for long except a feeling of well-being. When you have that, you don't need someone else to act as a mirror for your own ego." She grinned, teasing her neighbor. "Besides, I've always been afraid of communicable diseases."

"My God! Only you would think of that in the heat of passion! A businesswoman, through and through, even in the bedroom!"

"Now I am," she said, a thread of steel in her low voice. "But it took a long time to reach this point." Memories flashed through her mind quickly as she remembered the awful days early in her marriage when Thomas would scream at her for being so clingingly dependent upon him for everything, including her own happiness. Perhaps that was why he had turned to so many other women. Because once he let other women know that he was married and had a child on the way, he could then relax and enjoy their company. After all, other women could only demand sex from him—he wouldn't have to deal with Jessica's whining, desperate dependency. She shook her head to stop the flow of thoughts. But that was way in her past, over ten years ago. Another lifetime with another Jessica, just seventeen years old, who was as afraid of living life as she had been of losing Thomas; he was her tie to her past and the only security in her future.

"Out of curiosity, what happened to make you the business mogul you are today? You never talk much about your marriage or Marissa's father."

There it was, an invisible wall that closed out any thoughts Sheila might have read in her eyes. Apparently that was a closed subject.

"Nothing out of the ordinary. A too-young marriage that changed the course of three lives. It's an old story and one that borders on boring. I hardly remember it anymore."

"If it's such a dim memory, does that mean that you're once again ready to give men a chance?"

"Perhaps," Jessica said thoughtfully, then recognized the gleam in her friend's eyes. "Why, have you found another 'terrific' dinner partner you want me to meet?"

"Well," Sheila hedged, a telltale blush tinting her cheeks. "I do know this guy who works with Jack, and he's just gotten a divorce and is looking for, uh, companionship. I thought the two of you would hit it off."

"No thanks, Sheila." She chuckled wryly, unable to get mad at her friend's attempt at matchmaking. "But if I ever decide to get involved with a man, it will be one of my own choosing, thank you."

"I'm not saying you should go to bed with him! I'm just asking you to dinner, next week, Thursday night at seven," Sheila begged, with bright brown eyes. "Don't say no, or you'll make me look like a fool."

"No," Jessica stated emphatically before continuing to explain. "Double no. I don't want to meet anyone new just yet. I've just found me, and I'm enjoying my own company right now. I don't need any complications in my life."

"That's what you think," Sheila said cryptically before gulping down the rest of her wine as she prepared to leave.

Later that night, as Jessica got ready for bed, she wondered at her friend's observations. Was she ready to plunge herself once more into the marriage market? She knew she had changed drastically since the days of her marriage. So much so that she wouldn't even recognize the girl she used to be. Perhaps, just perhaps, it was time for her to stop wrapping herself in the small, tight world she had made for herself and venture out among the living.

She probed her old wounds, testing to see if

the ache of losing Thomas was still there. But all she felt was an ancient symptom of failure without the shame.

It still hurt to realize how badly she had failed at her shotgun marriage, but if repeating that mistake would give her Marissa again, she'd do it all over. Besides, it wasn't just she who had failed, it was also Thomas. And there was an entire set of circumstances that had held them together even though the situation was out of their control.

Her thoughts tumbled back to that tumultuous time when she had changed from a carefree high school student to a newlywed, pregnant teenager.

She and Thomas had gone steady ever since her fourteenth birthday party. His golden good looks and wisecracking ways had endeared him to her from the first moment they met at the snack bar of a football game. Within a week they were spending hours on the phone, telling each other their most hidden secrets and thoughts. Their biggest problem was that both parents tried to keep them off the telephone long enough for other family members to use it.

As their dating became more and more serious, so did their ambitions in life.

"I'm going to become a doctor and make millions writing diet books," Thomas would say, only half kidding.

"And I'm going to own a dress shop, carrying only designer labels," Jessica would respond.

"And we'll live in a big house with a maid and housekeeper to help with our children. And we'll travel around the world. I always wanted to see Japan," he would state as if it were already a fact just by saying it aloud.

And they would kiss, then kiss again until suddenly Jessica would pull away, inhibited by her upbringing and her own fears.

"If you loved me you'd let me touch you more," Thomas used to whisper into her ear, a groan in his voice.

And at sixteen she didn't have an answer to his accusation.

Then one afternoon she had seen him walking another girl down the hall to his locker, his hand around her waist as he whispered something to her, and Jessica's heart felt as if it would break. She knew the girl's reputation and realized why Thomas was flirting with her, but it didn't help.

And finally, at a drive-in movie and after several sips of liquor from a bottle that Thomas had brought, she had given in. In the beginning, with the glow of love and liquor, she had wanted him as much as he had wanted her. But it hadn't been as thrilling as she had dreamed it would be. It hadn't even been fun. Shortly after, with the grown-up game of making love came the grown-up consequence: pregnancy.

They married at the insistence of both parents

and they never disputed the right or wrong of it. Within four months they had each lost their dreams of glory.

They both lived with her parents, Thomas continuing with school to finish up his senior year while Jessica stayed at home, growing bigger and lonelier. Fights became an everyday occurrence. Thomas stayed after school later and later, and when he did come home, he would do his homework downstairs in the kitchen, where they couldn't talk in private. She began questioning his every move, afraid of finding out that he was dating on the sly, yet more afraid of losing him to someone else. How could she compete with anyone in school when her stomach was swollen with his child?

She became more and more dependent upon him in her attempt to hold on to what had been. And he resented her clinging hands and whining words.

The final blow came when Thomas realized he couldn't go to medical school. The blame fell on her small shoulders as he whipped her with accusing words that stung with defeat and frustration.

She had childishly thought that if they could move out of her parents' home, perhaps all would be well. They finally moved one month before the baby was due, but the only thing accomplished was that Thomas no longer hid his contempt for Jessica, flaunting it when the other

18

boys came over to drink or talk. She was held up to ridicule; and still she stayed. Where else could she go?

Both parents knew things weren't right between them but assured her that after the baby was born everything would work out. But they didn't begin to realize how irreparable the damage was.

Thomas began going to night school, taking the subjects that would eventually get him into a good medical college. Marissa was born late one night and Jessica had only her parents for comfort and support. Thomas couldn't be found.

The marriage barely lasted two more years, with Jessica clinging tighter and tighter and Thomas resisting her hold with every bone in his body.

And when he finally walked out her door to live with his new girlfriend, she reached the depths of a new low.

She lived with her parents again for a year while she studied for a high school equivalency test, got her diploma, and began working on a full-time basis. It was a year of forced growing up as she pulled away from all the familiar things she had known. A year of growth that was more painful than her daughter's delivery had been. She resisted every inch of the way until her metamorphosis was complete.

She learned so many things that year. She

knew now that divorce was as traumatic as death. Perhaps even more so, because in death there was a burial that hid any taint of failure, but divorce was a badge that would accompany her for a lifetime.

Now, twelve years later, she owned a dress shop that catered to the wealthy. She and the mortgage company owned a beautiful large and well-furnished home on the right side of town near good schools and good neighbors. She had security. Dependent upon no man for soothing pats to her ego, Jessica was her own woman. And in raising Marissa to be the girl she was, Jessica had in some way rid herself of any guilt she felt for her disastrous marriage.

Thomas, however, had remarried two years after their divorce. He completed college but he never entered medical school. His ability to work hard never equaled his dreams or expectations. Now working for an insurance company, Thomas had three more children from his second marriage and had never ceased to blame Jessica for his bad start in life. He pointed to her own single existence, insinuating that not only couldn't she hold him, but she also couldn't hold any other man, which made his earlier treatment of her less condemnable. It couldn't have been any fault of his, after all, that the marriage didn't work out. Jessica just wasn't good marriage material.

She hadn't seen him in four years. Neither had

Marissa. And neither of them seemed to care. Poor Thomas.

Jessica turned out the light and snuggled into the deep warmth of her king-size bed. Perhaps it was time to begin dating once again. Her clinging-vine days were over and she was a strong, mature woman now, not a teenager who was frightened that her boyfriend might leave her.

She would call Sheila and tell her she'd be delighted to come to dinner. After all, a date wasn't the commitment of a lifetime.

The store was busy for this time of year. Jessica took care of her customers speedily, though she remembered that her clientele needed that special attention or they would just as easily walk out and buy a dress elsewhere.

Two evenings a week Jessica held etiquette classes in the back of her dress shop. Many of her patrons sent their children to them, hoping that they would cancel out the days on end of loud music, gum snapping, and peer-group influence. Along with the etiquette classes a small seminar was held on makeup and personal health care, which proved to be even more popular than Jessica had imagined.

Tonight was the beginning of a new class.

"Mom?" Marissa played with the scalloped potatoes on her plate, one of her favorite dishes. She was obviously worried about something.

"What's up, doll?" Jessica continued to eat

slowly, knowing that whatever was bothering her daughter would soon come out.

"Susanna Pace's father is enrolling her in tonight's class. And she's worried. Can I come to the class tonight so she won't be so frightened?"

"What's Susanna frightened about? Surely you haven't painted me as a fire-breathing dragon, have you?"

Marissa made a face before smiling. "Of course I have. Don't you know you're not supposed to be nice? You're a mother, for goodness' sake, and I'm supposed to be able to gripe about you, not praise you!"

Jessica chuckled. "Then I'll be mean tonight. I'll growl more. How's that?"

"You're not the problem, Mom." Marissa turned serious once more. "It's Susanna's dad. *He's* a dragon, always filled with dire warnings, always waiting for something fatal and disastrous to happen. Why, he won't even allow her to wear makeup!"

"Perhaps she using too heavy a hand. We'll work on it," Jessica promised, eating with one eye on the clock. She still had an hour before classes began.

"Humph," Marissa said. "According to him she should go into a nunnery. He won't let her do *anything!*"

"It's a convent, not a nunnery." Jessica corrected Marissa automatically. "Do anything like what?"

"Like go to the shopping center after school, have boyfriends over, wear makeup. You name it and she's not allowed to do it! Why, I bet if Susanna didn't fight hard enough for it, he wouldn't even let her wear jeans!" Marissa had a definite flair for the dramatic.

"And you want to tell him how to raise his own child?" Jessica put her fork back on her plate and contemplated her daughter. She had a feeling she knew what was coming.

"No," Marissa spoke in a rush. "I want you to tell him. He'll be there tonight. He's escorting her there," she said, obviously disgusted that a fifteen-year-old should have to be escorted anywhere.

"I won't promise anything, but I'll see what I can do," Jessica said, knowing the discussion would be endless if she didn't stop it now. "But the man has a right to raise his child as he sees fit."

"I knew you would help!" Marissa gave her a big smile, her dimples once more peeping out. She ignored her mother's last sentence. After all, what did men know about raising girls? Her own father couldn't even remember her birthday!

Garner Pace stood at the entrance of Madison's, watching with pride as his lovely blond daughter almost ran to the back of the shop in her hurry to join her friend. She promised to be an even prettier girl than her mother had been, with taffy-colored hair and light green eyes. He only hoped he could instill in her the moral values her mother had so sadly lacked. Automatically he straightened his spine at the thought of the woman who had been his wife for six calamitous years. It didn't bear thinking about anymore. Flogging himself for the past was one thing he no longer did, making a concerted effort to block all thoughts concerning her. Over the years he had succeeded, with minor exceptions, such as this one, when his daughter squeezed his heart with the reminders of his own youth.

It hadn't been easy raising Susanna, but it had certainly been worth it. She had grown into a charming teenager who was his friend and companion in his loneliest moments. She was the one person who made him continue on his path when everything else seemed to work against him.

But recently she had begun to chafe at the bit of parental control, arguing that she was more adult than he gave her credit for. She couldn't understand that he had once had problems similar to hers and might have learned some answers by personal experience. He firmly believed that too much freedom was the downfall of teenagers. After all, look at the path her mother had taken.

He walked farther into the store, reaching inside his jacket pocket for his checkbook, his eyes now focusing on the beautiful brunette he guessed to be Marissa's mother. He knew all about Marissa and her mother; Susanna had given glowing accounts of them at almost every evening meal for the past two weeks. Marissa could do this, do that, and her mother was understanding and wise and wonderful and smart and single. His usually full lips thinned. How does a father compete with that?

"Mrs. Madison?" He reached the cash register and drew her attention away from the giggling horde of girls clustered in a corner as they pawed through the small rack of clothing put aside for a wardrobe consultation class.

"Yes?" She turned, and he was startled by the color of her eyes, a pale hazel that seemed to pick up the hue of the blue silk blouse she was wearing. Her skin was flawless, even at close range. The fluorescent lighting brought out the golden-red highlights in her lustrous dark brown hair. She was younger than he expected, perhaps thirty at most.

"I'm Susanna's father, Garner Pace. I'd like to pay you for the class." His voice was clipped, abrupt, and abrasive.

"Certainly. If you'll just make it out to Madison's and take one of the brochures on the counter. The class will be over at nine this evening, if you care to return then to pick up Susanna," she answered, equally cool. The man before her was such a compelling figure that she barely noticed

25

the girls frantically waving from the corner to remind her of her mission. "Or, if you like, I'll be glad to drop Susanna off when Marissa and I leave. We'll have her home before nine thirty."

"No, thank you. I'll wait." His cold tone of voice told her what he thought of her offer.

"Then I'm afraid you'll have to wait outside the building, Mr. Pace. Your presence during the class would only make the girls uncomfortable, and I won't be able to get them to open up with me." She was considerate but firm in her request. Her eyes focused somewhere over his right shoulder. He was so good-looking, she had to keep herself from staring. He wore white tennis shorts with an Izod pullover shirt in a deep blue that matched his eyes. Over his shoulders he had slung a blue and white warm-up jacket that accentuated the breadth of his chest.

"I see." His brilliant blue eyes took on a dark, stormy look. "In that case I'll wait in the car."

"As long as you're not parked directly outside the window, I see no problem." If he thought for one minute she was going to change her policy, he was sadly mistaken.

"Since I'm paying for something I'm not sure is worth the price, could you tell me exactly what you teach?"

Jessica took a deep breath, noticing at once that his penetrating gaze had shifted from her face to her breasts as they rose and fell in agitation. So that was the kind of man he was. What was good for the gander was fine, but the goose went under a different set of rules. It was perfectly all right for her to be a woman, but not a businesswoman.

"Etiquette has changed a great deal since you and I grew up, Mr. Pace, and a new, informal but also very specified type of etiquette has emerged. I instruct young women in social and dating etiquette for today's times—good grooming, posture, and telephone and table manners. The last class is devoted to clothing—how to combine and contrast your wardrobe, and how your clothes tell what kind of a personal image you present."

"Oh, and what are your clothes supposed to be telling me?"

"My dark-colored blouse is expensive, therefore I make a nice income. My tailored skirt tells you I'm functional, as do my rather plain pumps. My hose define a pair of fairly well-shaped legs that carry me around the store to do my work efficiently. And the buttons on my blouse are buttoned almost to the neck, which is supposed to tell you that I don't like men staring to see what is underneath my garments." Her voice was soft but the message was very loud and clear.

For the first time since entering the store, Garner Pace smiled, and his stern face was transformed with charm.

"Then you noticed my . . . interest?"

"Because I'm a woman doesn't mean I'm blind. It also doesn't mean that I like to be looked upon as a sex object."

Suddenly his smile turned into a dark-browed scowl. "Then you're the exception to the rule, Mrs. Madison." His emphasis was on the Mrs.

"And as I'm sure Susanna has mentioned, you also know I'm divorced. That doesn't make me eligible for the marketplace any more than it does you." She raised an eyebrow at him before turning her back and clapping the girls to attention, silently dismissing him from her presence, if not her mind. He disturbed her.

The first class went smoothly. The girls were giggling but receptive, finally opening up to voice problems they had run into at various social functions and wanted to be prepared for the next time. Two hours passed very quickly, and at nine the girls disappeared almost as quickly as they had arrived.

Jessica and Marissa folded the chairs and put away the blackboard, checking to make sure everything was ready for the next day's work.

"Did you get a chance to talk to Susanna's dad?" Marissa asked as she folded the last chair.

"I said hello to him and was able to give him a rundown on the classes," Jessica said dryly. "But I don't think Susanna's father had a very good opinion of me. Don't expect me to change the wisdom of his opinions." She remembered his dark blue eyes roaming her slim figure, and a small chill of reaction trembled at the base of her neck before running down her spine. "He's a hard man," she muttered almost to herself.

"That's what Susanna says, but she also says that when he's not caught up in business he's really wonderful." Marissa made a face. "He looks like the devil to me, all dark and angry and cold. I don't care if he is good-looking for an older man; he scares me!"

Jessica smiled at the phrase *older man,* having already guessed Garner's age to be around thirty-five. Even though his attitude was cold and impersonal, she knew he was probably a virile man, and reeked with sex appeal in his casual but impeccable attire. And from the piercing look he gave her, Jessica would guess that his nights were only as lonely as he wanted them to be. Most single women she knew would give their eyeteeth to climb all over his well-formed body in the hopes of catching him for a lifetime.

But not her.

He reminded her too much of Thomas; he was too good-looking, with charm abounding when he desired to turn it on, and not enough depth to wade in at knee level.

His eyes had silently informed her: I want you. But his attitude told her that he would make love and walk away, unharmed and uninvolved, leaving devastation in his wake. He would walk all over a woman if she let him, and most would.

"Mom?" Marissa brought her back to the present.

She smiled, chasing away emotions she hadn't encountered within herself in years, and didn't want to deal with now. "I'm sorry, what?"

"I said, now do you see Susanna's problem? Isn't he old-fashioned?"

"No, I don't think so. I saw concern and pride when he looked at her, not rigid indifference."

"Well, Susanna sure felt out of place not even being allowed to wear mascara and lipstick when she's out with the girls!"

Jessica's brow creased. "Wait a minute. Susanna always wears a little makeup." She hesitated, realizing what Marissa was getting at. "Except tonight."

Her daughter had the grace to look sheepish. "Well, she usually borrows mine and puts it on at school, then washes her face before *he* gets home."

Jessica looked stern. "I don't want you lending your makeup to Susanna again. Not until she has her father's permission. Understand?"

"Yes, ma'am." Marissa gave a sullen look, but it was wasted on her mother. Jessica stood, keys in hand, her hazel eyes filled with faraway thoughts.

Garner Pace's eyes seemed to follow her to the parking lot and into the car. No one could ever call him bland, she thought ruefully, but was able to put him out of her mind as she drove home and mentally went over her list of things to do tomorrow.

CHAPTER TWO

Jessica accepted Sheila's offer of dinner and had a pleasant evening with her "date," Arnie King. Sheila's husband, Jack, a hefty, jovial man, played the host and bartender to the hilt. The boys were relegated to the den and out of the adults' way and all progressed peacefully.

When the evening was over Arnie offered to walk Jessica to her door. She liked him well enough as a dinner partner, but knew that what he had in mind wasn't quite what she wanted. Good night kisses were often just payment for favors, and she had passed the stage of being impressed with someone so blatantly wanting her. But she acquiesced when she saw the gleaming challenge in Sheila's eyes. Sheila had probably made a bet with Jack that she wouldn't allow it and Jessica had been put in the spot of proving her wrong.

But her hunch as far as Arnie's designs on her were right. They had barely reached the front door when he made his move, one arm slipping around her waist while the other began fervently roaming her back. His lips came down hard and wet, repulsing Jessica immediately. But when she tried to retreat, he only held her tighter.

"Arnie, please." She heard a car door slam across the street. God, she'd die of embarrassment if one of her neighbors saw this scene. She struggled harder.

"You're so wonderful, Jessica. So beautiful. Can't I come inside for a nightcap? I don't want the evening to end. Let's go inside. I promise you, you won't be sorry."

"Let go, please. Now." From out of the corner of her eye she saw a tall shadowy form crossing her lawn. Oh, no, not him! Yet even as she cringed at the thought of Garner Pace catching her in an adolescent wrestling match, some impish part of her couldn't wait to see what he'd do.

"Aw, come on, Jessica," Arnie persisted. "Don't be so uptight. If it's your daughter you're worried about, she should be in bed by now anyway."

"I'm afraid Mrs. Madison has some business to attend to first." A cold rough voice spoke from the darkness of the front walk. Jessica almost laughed at the look on Arnie's face as he sized up Garner Pace, but she thought the better of it and kept quiet.

"Who are you?" Arnie muttered.

"Mr. Madison," Garner lied smoothly. "Please, get your hands off my wife."

Arnie looked down at her, obviously not believing the stranger. "Is this true?"

"Yes," she lied with ease, amazed at her decision to play along.

"I thought you weren't involved," he accused.

"You were wrong." Garner stood, hands at his side, watching the other man squirm under his stare.

"Is that true?"

"Yes," she lied again.

His hands dropped away from her body and she was able to breathe again. "That's a dirty trick, pretending you're single when you aren't," he muttered, before turning away and walking back across the lawn to the Hamiltons' house.

"I probably could have handled that myself but thank you," she said stiffly, feeling awkward now that Arnie had gone. What was Garner Pace doing here anyway? She was about to ask him when he spoke.

"Before you misunderstand, I ought to tell you that I didn't do it for you, Mrs. Madison. I've been sitting in my car for hours waiting for you and I need to discuss Susanna with you now. I didn't have time to watch you play games with that overgrown boy."

Her spine stiffened. "Oh, really? For your information that overgrown boy was playing his games all by himself. I wasn't leading him on. And it's hardly my fault you've been waiting, since I certainly wasn't expecting you."

She turned and unlocked the door, stiffly ushering him into the well-lit entryway and back into the large two-storied den. Placing her purse on the plush tan couch, she turned and faced him.

"What can I do for you, Mr. Pace?"

He was slow in answering, his eyes taking in the sum total of her figure. "Do clothes still speak, Mrs. Madison?"

Not quite understanding what he was getting at, Jessica slowly nodded her head.

"Very well, then I say the light wine color of your dress is just two shades from being the deep red so many women of the evening wear. The low V neckline tells me you're pleased with the roundness of your breasts, while the long sleeves ask me to believe you're demure and shy. Your open-toed sandals say you're a sensualist, earthy. Your dark hair is loose and flowing, begging some man to run his fingers through the thickness of it." His voice was low, husky with feeling. "No wonder your friend was confused by your signals." His eyes seemed filled with a deep emotion.

And Jessica knew which emotion she had triggered. It was shining brightly in his eyes. She also knew that he might be right about her outfit and herself, but she certainly wouldn't admit it for the world.

"What did you need to discuss with me that would make you lie so blatantly, Mr. Pace?" She would keep a firm rein on this conversation if it killed her. Her blood ran fast through her system, making her skin blush to a rosy hue.

He stared at her a moment more before taking a leisurely seat in the large wing chair against the window. "You're interfering with the raising of my daughter." His voice proclaimed they were now back to the original line of business.

She followed suit and sat down on the edge of the couch, wishing she had his control. Why did she let him get to her this way? "Oh? And how is that?"

"Through your daughter. She's been lending my daughter makeup, which is strictly against my rules. I came home early tonight and caught her with it painted on her face. When we finally got it off, she told me that Marissa had loaned it to her in school today. I want it stopped immediately."

"Susanna is fifteen, right?" Jessica knew the answer but waited for him to nod his head. "Then certainly she's old enough to wear a little mascara and lipstick."

"Not if I don't allow it."

"Don't you think you're being just a trifle old-fashioned?"

"No." He gave no explanation and expected no arguments.

"But surely a girl of fifteen needs to learn how to handle herself now, while she's still being governed. And if you don't allow her to experiment intelligently, how will she ever learn?"

"I'm not asking you to convert to my rules, Mrs. Madison. I'm telling you to inform your daughter not to do it again." He was implacable.

"And I'm telling you that if Susanna doesn't get it from Marissa, who knows how to apply it, then she will just borrow from someone else. You can't stop her from growing up, much as you would like to."

"You're no expert on what I would like or not like to do, although I'll give you full marks for guessing what was on my mind the other night. It takes experience for you to have read me so quickly, but I don't want my child getting mixed up with that kind of experience."

Jessica sat back and curled her arm around the side of the couch. Her temper was brewing, but she made herself answer his accusation with as much finesse as possible. Garner Pace was not going to get the best of her simply because she lost her cool.

"First of all, Susanna is not a child, and you're kidding yourself if you believe she is. And second, I resent the implications you've made ever since you met me. Since you know even less about me than you do about your own daughter,

I see no reason to carry this conversation any further."

He ignored everything but the reference to his daughter. "I know Susanna very well, and she's not a disobedient child." He used the word purposely. "Marissa must have talked her into this."

"On the contrary. Peer pressure is a powerful motivator. If Susanna is the only one in school not allowed to wear makeup, then she'll be ostracized simply because she doesn't conform to the teenagers' idea of normal. I think you might look to yourself and see if you're not prejudiced by the type of women you know personally. But don't judge your daughter by their standards."

A brilliant look flashed through his eyes, and for a moment she thought she saw pain, but it was gone quickly.

"And what type of women am I supposed to know?" he questioned with a deadly low voice.

"The kind that are more flesh and flash than anything else."

"How quickly you condemn."

"No faster than you," was her comeback.

A gleam of admiration lit his eyes. He leaned forward, casually clasping his hands between his knees as he stared at her.

Suddenly Jessica felt terribly uncomfortable. Her uneasiness had vanished, leaving a myriad of confused feelings in its place. She leaned back farther, as if to escape his intense blue-eyed gaze.

"How old are you, or is that question too personal?"

"Not at all," she said calmly. "I'll be thirty-two."

"How unusual," he muttered. "Most women would say they were thirty-one, not wanting to credit another year too quickly." His eyes narrowed and she could almost see the wheels of his mind clicking away. "Child bride?" She could hear the smirk in his voice.

"Yes, as a matter of fact."

He sat a few more seconds in silence. She shifted her position on the couch, wondering how she could get him out of her home without a scene. His voice startled her out of her reverie.

"With you so young and Marissa fifteen, I'd say it was a forced marriage."

"Mr. Holmes! Such a clever deduction!" She didn't see any reason to deny it. It wasn't a fact to be proud of, but she certainly didn't bear the shame by herself.

"Most marriages that young began in the back seat of a Chevy."

Now she was angry. She answered with all the dignity she could muster, refusing to apologize to a stranger for a mistake made in another lifetime. "It was a Dodge. The front seat. And I'd go through the hell of it again for Marissa."

"How commendable."

"It's time for you to leave, Mr. Pace. Take your stuffed shirt elsewhere to be laundered."

Her voice shook with anger, but most of all she was embarrassed. She had never discussed her past with anyone before. He had goaded her beyond her limit or she wouldn't have done so now.

Garner Pace heaved a sigh. "Look, I had no right to throw stones. Please accept my apology. I didn't intend to insult you in any way." His sincerity soothed her taut nerves, but still she was wary.

"I accept." She stood up, telling him the conversation was over.

"Have dinner with me tomorrow night."

His invitation took Jessica completely by surprise. She couldn't think of a single thing to say. Slowly she shook her head from side to side.

"Please," he tacked on as an afterthought.

Still she couldn't speak, and continued to shake her head.

"Say yes and I promise I'll behave myself. I'd like to discuss a few of Susanna's problems with you. Since you're such a shining light on her horizon right now, you might be able to help me understand her better." His last plea finally unlocked her tongue. "Because you are so young a mother, you seem to relate well to a teenage girl's problems. Better than I ever could."

"Why?" She was still shocked. "You don't even like me." She had to clear her throat, giving away the tension that filled her body from head to toe.

"That's not true." It was as if his confession were forced from his lips.

Before her head began shaking from side to side again, she found her mouth forming the slightly breathless words, "All right."

"Good. I'll pick you up at eight." He stood abruptly and began walking to the door, but when he reached the threshold of the den, he turned and flicked his glance around the peach, golden yellow, and tan room. "You've done a beautiful job of decorating. It looks just like a family home should, yet it carries a great deal of style."

Jessica stood on not too sturdy legs, still stunned by his direct approach. "Thank you."

"You're welcome." His smile was very attractive. "See you at eight." He quickly walked to the entryway and opened the door. Jessica was right behind him. "And lock the door after me. I don't trust Casanova to stay away after I leave."

She grinned as she remembered the look on Arnie's face. He had had all the symptoms of having his favorite piece of candy stolen from his grasp. "I will," she promised softly.

And she did.

Jessica trailed around the house, turning off all the lights and large ceiling fans that quietly whirred as they stirred the air. Slowly she walked up the stairs, her mind occupied with Garner.

41

All her instincts told her he was dangerous, yet for some reason she felt sorry for him. It didn't make sense. Perhaps she shouldn't go to dinner with him. He was just too masculine. Smiling once more, she reminded herself that the opposite of that was what Marissa called a wimp, and she certainly didn't want to associate with that type either.

No, she would go with him this once. But then she would not see Garner Pace again. He was just too menacing a figure to trifle with, and she had learned the hard way that playing with fire always left scars. He was not a man to take lightly, for he seemed the type who could cut people to ribbons within a minute's notice and never look back to see the damage he had wrought. Look at the way he'd interrogated her about her marriage.

She ignored the fact that she had wanted to go out with him so badly she could taste it. Just once. Despite his short attack on her this evening and for reasons she refused to delve into, Garner Pace made her feel extremely feminine. It felt good. For the first time in fifteen years she felt excited over a date.

"Do I look okay?" Jessica pirouetted in front of a pajama-clad Marissa. The full skirt of her dress shimmered with iridescent blue highlights as she twirled around.

"Wow, Mom, that's a knockout. Is it new?"

Marissa threw another kernel of popcorn into the air and caught it in her open mouth, her large brown eyes managing to continue to focus on Jessica.

"I just got it in and decided to try it on," Jessica answered, glancing at the mirror over the T.V, checking the neckline to make sure it was high enough. This dress would tell him she was feminine but wasn't in the market for games adults play, she hoped.

"I just hope Susanna's dad appreciates that you look so great. He seems like such a stick-in-the-mud, even if he did finally let Susanna wear some makeup today at school."

Jessica grinned. "Oh, he did, did he?" She grinned at the memory of them sitting practically knee to knee and badgering each other about teenagers' makeup. "Well, that's good. Now let's hope Susanna doesn't overdo it."

The persistent chime of the doorbell signaled his arrival. When she opened the door Garner Pace's eyes widened in undisguised appreciation before his deep gaze once more caressed the becoming blush that highlighted her cheeks. "You're beautiful, you know."

"Thank you. So are you," she answered, unaware of her choice of adjectives.

He smiled in return. "Are you ready?"

"Yes."

She gave Marissa a quick kiss on the nose, admonishing against horror movies and late bedtimes, and he guided her toward a deep burgundy two-seater Porsche.

"Lovely," she murmured as he opened the door.

"That's my line."

She gave a provocative glance over her shoulder. "It may be, but I'm speaking about the car."

He slipped into the driver's seat and backed down the driveway with a dull roar.

The restaurant was one of the most elite in Shreveport, the clientele known to drop several hundreds of dollars for a meal. Jessica had been there only once before, acting as a commentator for a luncheon fashion show. Her eyes scanned the small tables set in alcoves and corners, her smile deepening as she recognized one of her customers wearing a dress from her shop. They followed the maître d' as he ushered them to their table. He seemed to know Garner always sat there. When they were seated and had ordered both wine and dinner, she asked him just that.

His brows rose, surprised at her observation. "Yes, I sit here most of the time. How did you know?"

"Just a lucky guess." Her eyes twinkled at him. Was he the only one who thought he could play detective?

"You surprise me," he murmured, looking at her as if she were a puzzle he had yet to figure out. "Normally a woman of your beauty isn't concerned with others and their habits as much as she is with herself. Yet, you're a good businesswoman, if your shop is anything to go by, and an excellent mother, if Susanna is any judge, and now you show a keen sense of observation."

"My, my, this is my day for flattery. My horoscope said it was, and I didn't believe in the stars." She wiped away his compliment with teasing, suddenly afraid of becoming serious.

"The difference between flattery and truth is a lie. And I wasn't lying. Somehow I don't think I could win you over with flattery."

"Win me over to what?"

"To my bed." His voice was calm but filled with meaning as he stared at her, watching her reaction to his words.

Jessica stared at the candle on the table before once more looking up at him, a steel thread of determination glistening in her hazel eyes. "Don't let what you know about my marriage fool you. I don't go to anyone's bed but my own."

He ignored her first sentence completely. "That's fine with me. I don't care whose bed we make love in."

"You're wrong. It matters a lot. I don't go to bed just because a man asks me to. In fact, I don't go to bed with men at all."

"Why? Is there something in your makeup, some quirk that I don't know about?" His meaning was clear.

"No. I just don't happen to care for sex. Carefree and casual as today's society is, it has nothing to do with my own scruples."

"But you're a—" he began only to have her interrupt him.

"A divorced woman? And I should be hungry for a man's touch?"

He had the grace to look just a little embarrassed. "I wasn't going to put it that way."

"Any way you say it, the meaning is still the same." Suddenly she felt deflated. So he was the same as the others.

"Jessica . . ." He hesitated a moment, then took her pliant hand in his, staring down at the long, tapered fingers, his thumb circling the finger that had at one time worn her wedding band. "I know that in your case that's not true. But don't blame me because many women do like carefree sex. Your attitude is at least unusual."

She didn't doubt his sincerity, but the tone of bitterness she sensed puzzled her.

"Can we change the subject?" she asked softly, wanting to replace the despondency that had fallen upon them with a cheerier topic.

"Sure, as long as you'll consider going to bed with me sometime in the future."

"I thought we came here to discuss Susanna?" She grinned, knowing he was teasing now.

"I lied," he answered quickly. "I really came here to feast my eyes on you."

46

"In that case, you'll die of starvation quickly. There's not enough of me to feed a man of your appetite."

The rest of dinner was casual. He asked her to call him Gar and she did, his name tripping off her tongue as if it were the most natural thing in the world. She loved the sound of it, the taste of it as it left her tongue. His own intimate glance told her that he loved to hear her say it.

Garner drove home slowly, and each of them was quiet as they savored the last minutes of their evening together. Jessica felt the thrill of anticipation as the time for his good night kiss neared. For the first time in years she wasn't dreading that particular end to an evening. She was a teenager again, free and alive and filled with all the wonders and doubts that were part of dating someone one was particularly fond of.

Garner turned the motor off but made no move to open the door. His eyes strained in the darkened interior of the car, seeking Jessica with heightened intimacy. His hand came out and brushed her cheek, sending a heated wave through her body.

"Thank you for a wonderful evening," he said huskily.

She smiled. "That's my line," she reminded him.

"And my line is Do I get a good night kiss?" he teased in the same rough, sandpaper voice.

His lips came gently down on hers, erasing her words away before they were uttered.

She clasped her arms trustingly around his neck, feeling the muscles in his shoulders bunch as he felt her touch. Her fingertips teased the back of his hair, running her nails lightly through to his neck before repeating the action again. His grip on her waist tightened, his lips clinging even more, his tongue foraging through the softness of her mouth to seek an answer to his suddenly awakened need. He slowly moved his hand up to rest finally on her breast, his palm filled with her flesh.

A slow, deep moan echoed in her throat and she didn't know if she was protesting or asking for more. His thumb flicked past her nipple, causing it to spring into a bud waiting for his next sensuous move.

Finally he pulled away, his breathing as heavy as hers.

"Let's go inside," he ordered in a rasping tone.

Then suddenly she remembered where she was and stiffened. "No." She stilled the hand that held her breast, placing hers over his. "This is good night, Gar."

"After your response to a single caress, you can turn me away?" His derision was apparent and worked like a slap in the face. "Lady, you need to be made love to. Whether you know it or not, your body is crying out for love just as much as mine is."

"Maybe so. But I have control over my body, and what I say goes." She moved away, her hand reaching for the door handle. "Thank you for a nice evening, but I think it would be better if we didn't see each other again except through the children's activities." Her voice was dead, a complete monotone.

"What are you made of? Steel? How can you turn making love on and off just like that? Or is this all a game to you?" His eyes narrowed on her, searing her with the heat of his glance.

"Are you telling me that you love me?" she questioned him, her voice rising in incredulity.

"I'm saying that I'd love to make love to you," he corrected her, as if talking to a slow child. "Come off it; you've been around long enough to know that I want you."

"Funny. It sounds so funny. Age is supposed to grant me wisdom." Her eyes locked with his in the dark car. "But I don't have the wisdom to cope with you, Gar. And now I'm suddenly glad I don't. This is one little fish you'll have to chalk up as getting away. But don't worry, there are plenty of women out there in the ocean who are ready to be hooked and would be more than happy to warm your bed. I just won't," she promised determinedly.

As she stepped out of the car and onto the sidewalk, she heard his muttered response.

"Oh, yes, you will, Jessica. Let's just see how long you can hold out. You're too responsive to last the long siege."

She ignored him and walked to the door, inserting her key and closing it behind her. She didn't hear the sound of his engine until her hall lights flicked on. He had waited for her to reach the safety of her home before roaring off into the night. She leaned against the door, her trembling legs unwilling to carry her any farther until she caught her breath.

Slowly she walked around the house, checking the lights and doors and windows. Then she reached around the wet bar and poured herself a stiff glass of brandy, swirling it around the big-bowled glass as she curled up on the couch in the unlit room.

Gar had touched her emotions tonight. He had said so many little things that gave his personality away. His disenchantment with women must have stemmed from his marriage, for he had hinted that it hadn't been a pleasant experience. And now he seemed to treat women like sex objects rather than people. Women were to be admired for form and figure but not to be consulted on any other basis. They were supposed to be used, yet tonight she knew he had enjoyed their stimulating conversation, had sometimes even been surprised at her knowledge and sense of humor. She could have sworn he had had as good a time as she had—until his kiss.

But not only his kiss had frightened her. His very touch had sent tremors she couldn't disguise through her body. And he had known. Confirmation had shone in his eyes.

She had been drawn to him more strongly than to any other man. All others seemed like children, and her own previously tumultuous emotions were shallow compared to what she had experienced tonight.

It frightened her.

Two hours later she put down her almost untouched brandy and headed for bed, achingly tired from her confused thoughts.

But her mind was made up. She had been right. She would not see Gar again. It was best for both of them. Although she doubted she could do much damage to him, Garner Pace had the power to change her entire way of life.

CHAPTER THREE

Jessica made a concerted effort not to think of Garner Pace. However, it wasn't as easy as she had expected.

Marissa and Susanna became as close as only teenage best friends can be, sitting in their rooms, whispering and giggling over the rock stars, other boys in class, and clothing. They were together every day after school, and when they would join Jessica in the evening at the etiquette classes, Susanna always mentioned that her father was sitting outside in the car, waiting for her.

Apparently he still didn't want Jessica to drive Susanna home. Why? Because he didn't trust her driving, or her morals? She regretted ever admitting to him the circumstances of her marriage or Marissa's birth, mentally flogging herself for her candor. She had learned long ago not to expose herself to anyone's judgment. Yet, in one night she had opened a wound she had thought was closed and healed.

The fifth class was finished and Jessica was ready to dismiss the girls when the door buzzer went off. She glanced up, thinking it was an anxious parent, and her mouth opened wide enough to catch flies.

Thomas strolled toward her, very apparent appreciation of her slim but soft figure gleaming in his eyes. He didn't even bother glancing in the direction of the girls huddling together in a corner several yards away as they went through another rack of clothing.

"Hello, Jessica. Long time no see," was his only comment, as if he had not dropped out of sight four years ago.

Jessica took a deep breath as she finally collected her scattered wits enough to move forward to the cash register and out of earshot of the boisterous girls. Nodding her head, she said, "Hello, Thomas. What brings you here? Certainly not a pang of fatherly conscience at this stage of the game."

A glimpse of satisfaction glittered in his eyes. "Still bitter, Jessica?"

"No," she said calmly, uninterest apparent in her look. "I don't think about you enough to be bitter. What are you doing here?"

His eyes began darting around the room, as he suddenly felt uncomfortable. He had undoubtedly expected some reaction other than this. "I just thought I'd find out how the princess is doing. I am her father, you know."

"Oh, I know. I'm just surprised you remembered. And her name is Marissa, Thomas, or had you forgotten?"

"Please, don't pick a fight with me." He half turned, as if he were about to leave, but changed his mind when he realized she wouldn't stop him. "Haven't you missed me just a little? You used to, I remember." His same all-American smile was back in place. "I've missed you. Terribly."

She could tell he had thought his charm would win the day. According to the script he'd written, she was supposed to fall into his arms and replay one of the many scenes they had had in their marriage. He would be the prince and she would be grateful for the attention he had thrown her way. Her spine tingled with the knowledge and the irritation that went with it.

"I've been here all along. You could have visited. Or were you too embarrassed because you can't seem to remember her name, birthday, or the amount of the child support payments?"

"I didn't want to come knowing I couldn't even make the child support payments. You can understand that, can't you?"

"Hard times? You seem to support your wife

54

and other children adequately." As far as Jessica was concerned, she couldn't have cared less whether he ever came back into their lives or not.

He leaned across the counter, his face just inches from her own. "Finish up here and then come have a drink with me, Jessica. Please. I need to talk to someone, to you. You always did understand me."

"I'm sorry." Her voice was firm. She laid her hands on the counter to still their nervous clenching. Whether she wanted to admit it or not, his surprise entrance into her life had given her a shock. There had been a day, not so long ago, when she would have been thrilled to death if he had come back to her. And he knew it. But that day was history.

He clasped her hand from the counter. "Please?"

She twisted her hand, but he refused to relinquish it. It was as if he were holding it in an attempt to control her very actions and thoughts. Suddenly Jessica stopped struggling. She looked at him, really seeing him for the first time. Her first lover. Her only lover. And there was nothing, no feeling, no bitterness, no attractiveness to the man who was the father of her child. He was a total stranger, and one she had no wish to know better.

"Let go of my hand. Now," she said quietly.

She was so intent upon being set free she didn't hear the door buzz a second time.

"Are you ready to go, Jessica?" Gar asked smoothly, his larger body dwarfing Thomas's before either had noticed. "We promised the girls we'd get them home in time for that movie they wanted to see." The underlying tenseness in his shoulders told her he was just waiting for Thomas to make a wrong move, and he would quickly slip into action.

She gave a nervous grin in his direction. "Yes, thank you. I'll be ready in a minute," she confirmed, once more going along with his lie. Damn it! Was he always going to be around, getting her out of scrapes, pretending to be more to her than he was?

Thomas dropped her hand quickly, his expression freezing as he gave Garner a once-over. Before Jessica could move away, Thomas stuck out his hand toward the other man. "I'm Thomas Madison, Jessica's husband."

"Ex-husband," she corrected him quickly. "For the past twelve years."

He shrugged as if it made no difference.

Gar didn't shake hands. He didn't even bother to look in the other man's direction. Instead, he stepped around him and walked toward the girls as if Thomas were invisible. Thomas watched; the gleaming chill in his eyes and the red tinge on his cheeks and neck told of his embarrassment. He wasn't used to being ignored under any circumstances.

"Your boyfriend is a perfect match for you, Jessica. Cold as ice." Thomas's tone of voice brought back in vivid detail all the hurtful, cutting things he used to say to her when she didn't live up to his expectations. It was a shock to hear it again and be reminded of those awful, lonely memories that she thought had been locked up and stuffed in some dark closet of her mind forever.

Her legs trembled with the tension of her uncontrolled reaction. She glanced cautiously over her shoulder at Gar, realizing that although he had walked away, he had also made certain that he was still within hearing distance.

"Only where you're concerned, Thomas," she said with more conviction and control than she felt. "Tell me, can you recognize your own child in that group over there? Do you want to be introduced to Marissa, or would you like to leave quietly now? Either can be arranged, but the consequences of that decision are yours."

Hot air seemed to escape from his lungs. He stared at her a moment, then answered slowly. "I'll come back another time and see Marissa." His glance flickered over the girls without any gleam of recognition before glossing over Gar's lean frame and back to her. "And when I do, I'll talk to you again."

"I can't help you with your marital problems.

I'm not the answer." She had taken a stab in the dark for his reason to be there, and by his reaction she knew she had been right. She almost felt sorry for him. Emotionally he was still a teenage boy with visions of grandeur. He would probably never apply enough elbow grease to see those visions culminate into something solid and strong. Always the dreamer and never the doer.

Without another word he turned and left, his shoulders sagging.

Jessica herded the children out the door to the waiting parents, forcing herself to move limbs that seemed frozen. When all had left except for Susanna, Marissa, and Gar, she turned to face them, hoping she would be able to stand without collapsing for another minute or two.

"Ready?" Gar asked, his deep voice laced with concern.

"Please, don't be nice to me, Gar, or I'll cry all over your clean shirt." She gave a watery smile and turned to dim the lights, ushering the girls out the door.

"Horrors!" he muttered dryly, making her smile once more.

"Pizza! Pizza!" The girls sang, dancing a topsy-turvy jig on the shopping mall sidewalk as they waited for Jessica to lock up.

"I promised them a trip to the pizza parlor for dinner tomorrow," Gar explained softly, just behind her shoulder. He didn't have to touch her to let her know he was there; her nerve endings sang with awareness. An invisible built-in radar system told her of his nearness, her nerves tensing with excitement and pouring adrenaline through her system. She wasn't sure if she should fight or flee. Her intuition told her to run just as fast as she could, and in the opposite direction from Gar. But her heightened senses also enjoyed the danger of being close to him.

"I'm sure you'll enjoy keeping them occupied," she retorted shakily.

"Oh, no. I'm going to be busy keeping my date occupied. The girls can take care of themselves. Besides, what could happen at a pizza parlor that would get them in trouble?"

Jessica laughed out loud, her first spontaneous laugh all night. "Oh, boy, you are naive!"

"But I have you to teach me." His voice was low and husky, rasping against her spine.

"I'm sorry. You've got the wrong woman." Suddenly she had had more than she could cope with in one night. If he thought she was going to fall into his arms, he had another think coming.

He suddenly turned serious, his blue eyes stabbing her with intensity and a certain sympathy. "Stop jumping to conclusions. Don't look for implications where there are none. I'll let you know what's on my mind. I won't play word games, not with you." He took her elbow and walked her toward their parked cars. "I'll pick you both up around seven. Wear jeans and a sweat shirt, and a scuffed pair of sneakers. We're eating pizza, drinking beer, and playing games with the girls." He stopped, taking the keys out of her hand and unlocking the car door. "Understand?"

She saw the humor in it and grinned, saluting smartly. "Yes, sir!"

He and Susanna sat in their car until she drove off with Marissa. Once more he was making sure she was safe.

She hadn't been watched over in years, but the feelings he aroused by doing so were a total surprise to her. Usually she didn't care for protective men, but with Gar she felt warm, and wanted, and cared for. She also felt excited and alive. She smiled all the way home, nodding her head in all the appropriate places as Marissa rattled off the events of the day. She was only giving half a mind to her daughter's conversation. The other half was occupied with Gar's unusual reaction to Thomas.

Had he been jealous? Is that why he walked away without shaking hands? She didn't think so. Had he just been indifferent? She couldn't begin to tell the difference.

And Thomas. She had been more shaken by his appearance than she was willing to admit, even to herself. She didn't tell Marissa her father had been in the same room with her and hadn't wanted to talk to her. Why should she hurt what had slowly been healing over the years? No child wants to believe her father doesn't care for her, but Marissa had finally faced that fact and was adjusting well. And Marissa hadn't recognized him at all. Not that she should—she had only a dim memory and a few faded photographs of him. And she certainly hadn't expected to see him.

Why after four years would he expect a warm welcome? What could have prompted him to look her up now? Had she been right in assuming he had problems at home and had turned to the only other woman he had known? She didn't know. Perhaps he thought she would be willing to take up with him again. After their divorce she had certainly acted like it on more than one occasion. But Thomas had never had trouble finding a soft shoulder to cry on. And he was still as handsome and all-American as he had always been. Sandy-blond hair and sparkling blue eyes and tanned skin. Except now he had light but defined circles under his eyes and the faint beginnings of a paunch that declared that he hadn't bothered to keep himself in shape. He had looked tired, too, but it had been a world-weary tired—more from attitude than effort.

But there had been no question about the blatant look of desire that had gleamed in his eyes. That had done more to restore Jessica's self-confidence than anything else.

Years ago he had told her she looked big and ugly, and now he desired her. Once that would have made her ecstatic. But that was another lifetime. It was hard to remember it anymore. It seemed hazy, as if it had happened to someone else, not to her.

And she didn't want to see him again. Nor did she really want Marissa to see him. Marissa had painted her own lovely picture of her father, and the experience of seeing him as he really was might be too much for a vulnerable teenager to handle right now. He had no right to come into her life just when she had begun to take the lack of a father in stride.

By the time Jessica was ready for bed, she had decided she would put off Marissa's meeting with her father for as long as she could.

Her thoughts kept her awake far into the morning, tossing and turning with bitter churning emotions dug up from the past that had been better off buried.

Her final sleepy thoughts had to do with Gar. Although she knew she shouldn't, she also knew she'd go to the pizza parlor with him and the girls tomorrow.

Fool! her conscience proclaimed.

But her last memory was that, even after Thomas had left, Gar had never said a word about seeing him. Strange. Not a word. But she'd bet her bottom dollar that he'd say something tomorrow.

"I love your jeans and sweat shirt. It's the

most becoming ensemble I've seen in a long time," Gar teased as he jokingly leered at her over a stein of golden beer.

Jessica laughed. "I had to buy them this morning. K mart may never be the same. I couldn't find the right color, and the saleslady had to go in the back room and fight boxes for this."

"Hmmm. You'd think they'd have plenty. I thought steel-gray sweat shirts were in years ago."

"They were, but not with Smurfs on them," she retorted. "Smurfs bring the entire wardrobe up-to-date."

"I can tell you own an exclusive shop. I never would have noticed the colorful little elves. But now I'm tempted to run out and buy one of those sweat shirts myself." His teasing was light, his conversation as quick as hers. His taste in pizza was also similar: pepperoni, black olives, and mushrooms covered the entire thick whole-wheat dough. Not a bite was left when they finished, however; everyone had been ravenous tonight.

Gar glanced over at the electronic machines lined up against the wall. The girls were playing Pac-Man and several boys had lined up behind them, more to tease than to wait in line for the game.

He frowned. "Don't those guys have anything better to do?" he growled.

Jessica widened her eyes in pretended innocence. "Better than teasing girls? The only thing better than that is a football game or a car engine!" she replied. "Weren't you ever young?"

"Yes, and I remember the trouble youth led me into," was his grim answer.

"Ah, yes, the sins of the father come back to haunt the child."

His dark blue eyes once again focused on her. "How can you say you aren't worried after what happened to you? Or do you really think you were the exception to the rule?"

Here it came. She knew he would roll around to her marriage. "No. I wasn't the exception," she admitted. "But I wasn't as smart as this generation either. I've made sure that Marissa knows the effects that premarital sex can have on the rest of her life."

"And I bet she also knows that you'd do it again to have her. Perhaps she thinks she'll feel the same way," he argued.

"She knows better. Marissa didn't come out unscathed and remembers enough of my circumstances to realize the tragedy of a forced marriage, of a child who comes into life with a mother almost too young to cope." She didn't know why she took the time to explain this to him. With every word she only added more fuel that he could use to burn her better.

"You hope." He reached for his beer, a scowl still lining his brow.

"I know." Her voice was quiet but he heard her, stopping his beer glass halfway to his mouth as he stared at her through narrowed eyes. "But if you want to be judge and jury for something you know only the surface of, then I think it's time we did what I originally proposed and not see each other again. I don't need the guilt you assume that I should feel. I don't know how you coped with your mistakes in life, but I do know the extremely high price I paid for mine. I'll mete out my own punishment, thank you."

Her stomach was tied into knots, causing the pizza almost to rise in her throat. She had never been so disappointed or so frustrated before. If this was what dating was all about, then she could stay home and conduct her own post mortem.

His glass thumped on the table. "I'm sorry. That was uncalled for." He hesitated a moment, as if he were about to say something else. Instead, he asked, "Am I forgiven?"

She couldn't help it. She smiled. "Just this once, Gar."

They watched the girls play another game, Gar keeping a cautious eye on the teenage boys standing behind them.

"You know, you never said a word about Thomas," Jessica finally said.

He shrugged his shoulders. "What was there to say?"

"I don't know, but most people would have

acknowledged him in some way, either with questions or observations."

Once again Gar was evasive. "I just didn't see the point. You were upset already."

"Thank you," she answered softly.

This time he grinned lopsidedly and made her heart smile. "You're welcome."

"Gar," she asked hesitantly, gaining his attention once more. "You never talk about your wife. Is she alive?"

His look froze, shuttering closed. "No. She died six years ago."

"I'm sorry." She felt contrite in bringing up something that so obviously hurt him. Damn her curiosity!

"Don't be. She wasn't worth one damn tear." His voice was as cold and heartless as his expression.

Jessica was stunned by his words, unable to think of a thing to say. Her tongue suddenly tied, she turned and stared at the cartoons going on in the other area of the pizza parlor.

"Did I embarrass you?"

She shook her head from side to side, unable to answer.

"Carla and I got married at the end of my freshman year in college. I quit school and went to work part-time, finishing my degree at night. When Susanna was four, Carla walked out on both of us. We never heard a word from her again. When she died she was in the south of

France, a rich man's mistress. But she had already died for us years before her auto accident."

Unbidden tears welled in Jessica's eyes. He had had as tragic a marriage as she had. No wonder he was so bitter. Without thinking, Jessica reached across the table to rest her hand on top of his, offering comfort to a hurt that was still so apparent, even after all these years.

"I'm sorry, but for you and Susanna." Her voice wavered with emotion, empathy for his plight showing in her face.

"Don't be. I learned a lesson much like you did. I'll never marry again. Ever. I have Susanna. That's all that counts." It sounded like a vow. He didn't remove his hand, but his tone of voice told her of his detachment and she snatched hers away as if it had been burned.

Four times she had seen Garner Pace and three times he had cut her to the quick. When would she learn that her first impression was the correct one—stay away from him!

She searched for another, less painful topic. From now on, she silently vowed, she would keep things light and impersonal.

"What do you do for a living?" she asked, surprising him with her change of subject.

Suddenly she could see his shoulders relax and his face brighten. "I own a string of do-it-yourself retail stores."

"Oh, which ones?"

"Can-Do-It."

Her hazel eyes widened. "But that's a huge conglomerate!"

"No, it's still privately owned—by me."

"And do you practice what you preach?" she asked, a dimple showing at the side of her mouth.

"Of course."

"Good. Then can you fix the molding on a kitchen cabinet?" She had caught him completely off-guard. After the blank look left his eyes, he grinned disarmingly.

"Why don't you come to one of the stores and they'll show you how to do it yourself, for future reference, of course."

She chuckled. "Caught at my own game," she teased in a husky voice. "But thank you. I'll just hire a carpenter. I've tried to do things like that before and only wound up with bent nails and swollen thumbs. No coordination at all."

"Really? You could have fooled me," was his answer, and it made a light-peach tinge show up on her cheeks, glowing deeper with the intimate look he gave her.

Gar glanced down at his Rolex watch. "I think it's time we got the girls home and to bed. School tomorrow," he said, and she felt an unexpected wave of disappointment as she realized that the evening had come to an end.

With the exception of their overly personal

conversation, she had enjoyed the evening immensely.

The girls chattered in the back seat all the way home. Jessica listened with half an ear, her focus on Gar's lean hands as he carefully controlled the car down the streets of the neighborhood. This time they were in Gar's fawn-colored Cadillac. She wondered briefly if he had a car for every occasion.

Once he halted at a stop sign and looked over at her, his deep blue eyes darkening with an intimate message as they each read the desire in the other's eyes. A horn sounded behind them, making Jessica jump. The spell had been broken.

And she was glad. There was no sense in their relationship going any further. Gar was definite in his stand on a second marriage and all she could see ahead was a very rocky road to heartbreak.

She realized now that she was finally free of the shackles of bitterness that were born of her own marriage and ready to find and build a good relationship with someone. But Gar was nowhere near being ready for that same commitment. He was still hurting, and that would limit any relationship he had. He wanted only a playmate; that much was obvious. Jessica just wasn't the type to hold her own in that particular arena. She knew better than to try to change his attitude. After all, she had tried it before with Thomas and had learned only through pain that love can never be forced on someone, and commitment was the only rock she wanted to base a marriage or long-term alliance upon. She wanted to love and be loved.

Suddenly she felt very lonely.

CHAPTER FOUR

The week passed slowly, with Gar constantly intruding on Jessica's thoughts. She would be on the phone with an order and his face would flash in front of her, a teasing smile tugging at his full, chiseled mouth. Or she would be helping a customer and a word or two he had said in a low, rough voice would come back to her, making her blush with the tingling, intimate thoughts that accompanied the memory. She had to face the fact that she had gotten to know and like him too well. It was her own fault. Subconsciously she had been looking for a mate, and when she found someone who pleased her, he didn't want what she needed to have—commitment.

Gar was like a somewhat tamed tiger. Sometimes she could pet him and he purred, and at

71

other times he would bite. She never knew from minute to minute which he was going to do, and the danger excited her. At least that was the reasoning she used in the bright light of morning. The nights, just before sleep came, were different.

When the room was dark and she lay in her bed, her mind would play tricks on her, telling her Gar would come into the room in a minute. He would slide into bed next to her and take her in his arms. His hand would slip to one soft breast, and his deep, warm sigh would caress her cheek as he held her close to his firm, naked body.

Suddenly, sexual thoughts that she had buried deep in her subconscious over the years resurfaced, almost frightening her with their intensity. As soon as she remembered his words when he had declared he wanted to make love to her, her skin would quickly heat, her muscles tighten with pure, unadulterated desire. Deep in her abdomen a slow, spiraling warmth would invade her limbs. Most nights she tossed and turned, hoping that his absence would eliminate the constant ache for him that seemed only to grow with every passing day.

Still she refused to delve too deeply into her intimate feelings and thoughts, afraid of what she might find. It was better not to know. There was safety in ignorance.

By Friday night her nerves were wound too

tight to sleep, and even two glasses of wine wouldn't relax her enough to matter. She turned on the late programs on TV, hoping an old movie would do the trick, but to no avail. Gar's countenance was superimposed on every man's face. Gar's deep, penetrating voice echoed in every piece of dialogue. It was three in the morning before her head nodded and she slept—on the couch.

When she awoke, her head ached, her neck was stiff, and she wanted to cry. Why? Why after all these years of self-imposed celibacy would she now turn into a sex maniac? It didn't make sense!

She cursed herself for all kinds of a fool as she burned her tongue on her morning coffee. Muttering words of encouragement and small platitudes, she showered and dressed in her weekend uniform of shorts and a tube top. She tried whistling old show tunes, concentrating on the trills.

And when the knock came on the door, she was relieved. Perhaps it was Sheila for coffee. Sheila could take her mind off Gar. She knew it. Sheila could take her mind off anything because she had to concentrate so hard just to figure out what her friend was trying to say.

She opened the door and her hand automatically locked on the knob. Her heart began beating like a wild jungle drum, so loud that she was sure he could hear it. She stared at the man she thought her wishful thinking had conjured up.

Gar stood, tall and lean and tanned, on the front step. His slow, seductive smile was even more devastating than she had remembered. "Aren't you going to invite me in?" he teased, reaching toward the ground for a long metal box that looked like a tool kit. "If you don't, I won't be able to fix those cabinets you refuse to cope with."

Jessica tried to put a lightness in her voice. "Of course, come in." Her legs refused to move gracefully as she led the way through the den and into the kitchen. She could tell he was watching her as intently as she had stared at him in the doorway; the hair on the back of her neck stood, itching for him to soothe it.

"There they are." Her voice was light with happiness at seeing him again, and she tried to repress the smile that continued to tug at the corners of her mouth. Jessica pointed to the small cabinets under the kitchen sink. "The darn glue just won't hold the wood in place."

"Perhaps it's because you need finishing nails," he said dryly as he leaned down to examine them closer.

His dark hair caught and held the early morning sunlight, turning it a deep bronze. It looked healthy and clean, with a vitality all its own. She clenched her fingers into the palm of her hands.

"Would you like a cup of coffee?" Jessica couldn't think of another thing to say. Suddenly she was as tongue-tied as a teenager on her first date.

"I'd love one. Black, please." He spoke into the dark cavern of the cabinet, all his attention focused on the woodwork, until he glanced over his shoulder to where she still stood, staring down at him with an obvious, yearning hunger in her eyes.

Their eyes locked and Jessica felt herself hurtling through time to the upheaval of first love. The immediate rush of tender, loving emotions flooded her with feelings that shone from the depth of her wide hazel eyes.

"You're beautiful." His voice was almost a whisper, yet echoed through the room.

"Thank you," she said with all the childish sincerity of an honest answer. She couldn't think of anything else to say and really didn't want to bother. She just wanted to bask in the heat of his desire. His gaze was like a caress and she could feel herself responding to his magic. Her body sang with a song she hadn't thought to hear ever again. *I want you, I want you,* her blood hummed, and his gaze silently took up the same chant.

She had been wrong about first love, her mind told her, laughing at her naivete. With a flash of insight she knew that this was far deeper, far more powerful than she had first thought. This wasn't first love. This was real love. The love of a woman grown for an adult man. It was everything she had ever dreamed of and had never experienced.

Gar unfolded his lean body to stand over her, his hands reaching for the smoothness of her shoulders, as if they had to touch, to feel, to absorb, what he wanted so badly.

She searched his face, finding the commitment she had earlier ached to see, and slowly she smiled before reaching up to gently put her hands about his neck and bring his lips down to cover hers tenderly.

Their kiss held the promise of fulfillment. His arms came around to hold her waist firm in his hands, and drifted down to bring her hips into a tighter mold with his. His mouth was neither passionate nor hungry, rather like a man who has reached the clear liquid of precious water and knew he had to draw it out to savor the goodness of it.

Jessica's breasts flattened against the broad breadth of his chest, tingling with the awareness of him and begging to be touched. As if he read her thoughts, one hand came up to tease its tip to a peak of tender aching. Her warm blood coursed through her form, every drop seeking his body to reach a fulfillment it had not asked for in years.

A moan came from deep down, but Jessica didn't know if it was his or hers as she ran trembling hands down his back and across his shoulders to savor the sweetness of his flesh. She wanted to fade inside his skin, become invisible within him, and know his body as well as he seemed to know hers. She never wanted his kiss to end.

His tongue foraged through, seeking the small hidden crevices of her mouth, his lips moving slowly over hers. His body was slightly bent, better to accommodate her curves and softness with his own hard strength. And she could feel every inch of his response as she wiggled closer. Her hand cupped the strong contours of his rugged face, her fingers seeking the abrasiveness of his jaw.

Slowly the pressure of his lips released hers, just barely touching as if reluctant to part from the honey softness of her mouth.

"Jessica. I need you," he murmured seductively, his mouth moving just enough to make her stomach rise to a new, more tangible level of hunger for him.

"I need you too," she murmured back, her voice sounding like a whisper of night air.

"When? Now? I want you now." Still his lips hovered just above hers, neither of them able to break the physical contact first. His hand lightly roamed her breast, making it swell and ache for release.

"Whenever."

"Now. Where's your room?"

Neither was in a hurry to move.

"Upstairs, but Marissa's up there."

"I don't give a damn." His words were the first to show impatience. "I'll take you in the bathroom, or the living room, or here in the kitchen. I want *you,* not a room or a floor."

Jessica was still filled with an inertia, a slow-moving lethargy that flowed through her veins. His hands began traveling lightly over her body, one hand slipping to the inside of her thigh to feel the silkiness of her skin. A faint, soft sigh escaped her lips.

His breath was warm upon her skin. Without thinking, she allowed the tip of her tongue to caress the outline of his mouth, savoring the taste of him and tasting herself. It was a heady feeling to know that he tasted the same as she. An intimacy they shared together. He moaned, suddenly crushing her to him, all control finally breaking its leash and bounding away with both of them. His hands cupped her head to keep her closer to him as his tongue darted sensuous patterns in the hollow of her willing mouth.

They both heard footsteps on the stairs at the same time. It took all the willpower Jessica had to let go of him and take a step back, watching him watch her take gulps of air to calm her tattered nerves. A small part of her noticed with satisfaction that he did the same. A flicker of pain crossed his face before he bent down and began studying the cabinet door once more.

Just before Marissa reached the kitchen, he looked over his shoulder. "I'll get you for this," he threatened teasingly in a deep, growling voice.

Suddenly her heart was happy. "I hope you will," she said, in her voice the promise of other times and other places lighting up his eyes once more.

"Mom," Marissa called as she walked across the den to the kitchen. "Isn't there some way I could go with you to Dallas next week? I don't want to stay with that grouchy Mrs. Johnson!" Her voice almost ended with a wail, but was cut off quickly as she glanced down to see her best friend's father squatting on the floor in front of the kitchen cabinet. Her face flamed as she realized she had been caught whining in front of him. He was such a stuffed shirt already! "Hello, Mr. Pace. I didn't see you," she tacked on, quickly remembering her manners and hoping he would remember his enough to forget the tone of her earlier words.

His knowing eyes twinkled as he answered. "Good morning, Marissa. I'm fixing your mother's cabinet doors. They seem to be giving her a problem."

Jessica could tell he had something on his mind besides speaking to Marissa, but she didn't think it was the earlier scene. How could he control his emotions so well?

He busied himself with the loose piece of wood. But just as Jessica was going to address Marissa's problem, he casually asked, "And what are you going to Dallas for, Jessica? Business or pleasure?" His voice hardened almost imperceptibly on the word *pleasure.*

Jessica glanced at Marissa, wondering if she heard it too. She hadn't.

"I'm going on a buying trip for the shop this weekend. I do it four or five times a year."

"Oh, really? Well, I have to be out of town about the same time, but Marissa is more than welcome to stay at our home. My housekeeper would be delighted. That way she'd have someone else to cook for and also wouldn't have to worry about Susanna, since Marissa would be there to keep her company." His voice sounded so helpful, so innocent and pure. Why did she feel as if she were a canary who had just wandered into a cat's mouth, thinking it was a safe, warm place to hide?

Before she could file her thoughts into some type of coherent order, Marissa was doing an impatient dance, jiggling her arm at the same time. "Oh, Mom, please say yes. Please?" she implored. "You know I hate that Mrs. Johnson, she's such an old stick-in-the-mud. Besides, I wait on her hand and foot! She always says I'm younger than she is and makes me run errands up and down the stairs all the time! Please?"

"Well, if you're sure it's no trouble . . ." Jessica tried to see the situation logically, but Gar looked up at that point, the promise of other things to come in the glint of his eyes.

"I'm very sure," he said with confidence, implying more than just the answer to her question.

Without thinking the problem through, Jessica quickly made up her mind. "Then it's fine with me, Marissa. But you had better be good, or Mr. Pace won't ask you back again." There was a smile on her lips as she gave her daughter a hug, but her eyes were still on Gar.

She made a crisp tuna salad for lunch with a bowl of soup and light crackers with sharp cheddar cheese slices. Gar drank a cold, imported beer while she sipped on iced tea with mint.

They sat opposite each other, the house quiet except for the low tones of the stereo drifting through the house. Marissa had decided to ride her bike to Susanna's house and give her the good news.

Gar leaned back, finally full. "I don't think I've ever sat across from a lovelier lunch partner or eaten so much," he said contentedly, his eyes roaming her face with a tenderness that she could feel from across the table.

"I know," she said softly. "I feel the same way."

"Not even when you were married?" His question shocked her. She hadn't expected him to mention Thomas.

But she answered candidly. "We lived with my parents when we married. We were never alone. By the time we had a place of our own, it was too late. Our marriage had already been damaged beyond repair. It was something that never should have been."

Gar cocked his head, his deep blue eyes studying her. "Why?"

"Because we were too young and thrown into circumstances that were beyond our control. We hadn't learned to control ourselves, and there we were, trying to control our destiny. It was too much to expect."

"Yet some marriages last, even beginning under circumstances such as yours."

She nodded slowly. "Perhaps. Mine didn't." Her curiosity got the better of her. "And yours didn't last either. Why, Garner?"

"Because it take two. In my case, neither one of us tried. My wife wanted everything given to her immediately. She didn't want a house, children, a husband. She wanted love and romance and travel. Only I didn't know that until after the ceremony." His voice showed his disgust. "She couldn't even try, not even after Susanna was born."

"I'm sorry." She found herself apologizing, not for the breakup of his marriage, but for the hurt he still felt.

"Don't be." His voice was crisp with determination. "I found out the hard way never to be sorry for the past, but to learn from it."

"And what did you learn?"

"Never to marry again," he stated with conviction. "Do anything, but never marry again."

"Never?" She tried to keep her voice light but unformed thoughts that hovered in the back of her mind died a painful death with his words. Her emotions plummeted.

He seemed to understand her mixed feelings and tried to let her down gently. He shook his head. "Never, Jessica. I may love and I may make a commitment, but it won't be in the form of marriage. Marriage is for those who want to legalize children and property, not for those who want to love."

Jessica stared down at her plate, unable to see the strength of determination on his face.

He reached across the table and took her hand, his body leaning forward to capture her attention. "You see, if I married, I would have to bring that woman into my home. Susanna would then be under her influence. And if anything went wrong with that marriage, then I would not be the only one to suffer. Susanna would also be involved." His face hardened. "And Susanna has been hurt too much already. I'll never let anything hurt her again if I can help it. She's the best thing that ever happened to me. And a failed marriage is one of those things that can hurt her."

"You're still very bitter." Her voice was soft with a saddened understanding. She knew how he felt. She had been there once herself. Only now she realized that after the hurt was over, a healing process began. It took longer for some than others, but with time, new relationships, and confidence in oneself, it worked. He hadn't yet reached the point where he would be able to commit his love and his life and his body to another, giving total trust and help only to have it returned twofold from the right person.

He looked like a parent seeing a younger child express her far-fetched wishes. "Not bitter, Jessica. Realistic. What I don't understand is how you could even entertain the notion of remarriage. Haven't you been hurt enough to learn yet?"

"Yes. But I don't think I could explain it to you." She pulled her hand away from his and began gathering the silverware and dishes to take to the kitchen.

How could she explain that when love entered, only a total commitment on both sides could satisfy her? That when she loved someone, she wanted to be with them for always? That a piece of paper was really a declaration to the world that these two people would stay together and live their love in the open, where it would grow and produce more love in the sunshine of the future?

His hands stopped her as she walked around the side of the table. He took the dishes from her hands and placed them back on the table before bringing her down to sit on his knees, his arms encircling her waist and hips. "I'm telling you this, Jessica, because our relationship is growing and I want you to know how I feel, up front. I don't want you to dream of something that won't be. You're a good businesswoman, an excellent mother, and an understanding woman with a depth of insight that is hard to find today. I want us to see a lot of each other, be together, but I also want you to know where I stand, and why." His lips nuzzled the soft curve of her neck, sending chills down her spine. "I want you so much it hurts even to think about it, but I also want to share your wit and humor and intelligence. I've never told any other woman what I've expressed to you today. But you're different. Both of us should know the other's feelings before we become more involved. I don't want to deceive you, even unintentionally."

Her heart lightened with his words. Perhaps, just perhaps, there was a chance of changing his mind. With time . . .

His lips came down on hers and blotted out her unformed thoughts. She leaned back in the crook of his safe arms and wrapped her hands around his neck to hold him close, knowing that her love was strong enough for both of them right now. Later he might realize just how wrong his attitude was and change his opinions. After all, the future made anything possible.

Jessica glanced out the plane window occasionally as she flipped through the airline magazine and sipped a glass of white wine. She had dropped Marissa at Susanna's house and spoken to the housekeeper, giving her the key to the house in case of an emergency. She had given all her dire warnings to both girls while admonishing them to have a good time this weekend. She smiled to herself. She hadn't given them an easy task.

Gar had already left on his business trip. Susanna and the housekeeper had been vague about it, both saying something about Houston and a store that wasn't working out as well as he had hoped. They had his number in case of emergency, and now they had hers too. She had already told Gar where she was staying in case they lost it, so everything was well in hand.

She couldn't believe Friday afternoon had come so quickly. Gar had helped to speed the time by calling her at work every afternoon and teasing her with his low, husky voice as he propositioned her outrageously. But at night, when the etiquette classes were over, he was no more than friendly, saying nothing that even hinted at a deeper relationship. No one would have known that he had just called that afternoon and asked her if he could kiss her ankles in the heat of love, or if she minded that the small of her back was probably going to be her most erotic spot for him. Then, just after the news at night, and after Marissa had gone to bed, he would call once more, explaining in detail just how much he wanted to make love to her, with instructions on what he wanted her to anticipate. The rest of the night she would toss and turn as her body responded to his words.

She smiled again. Perhaps she needed this time away from him just so she could catch up on her sleep.

However, the one thing that puzzled her was that he had made no move to actually get her into his bed. It was a good thing, though, because she wasn't sure how strong her resolve was. He was wearing her down daily, and she thought he knew it. Maybe he didn't; but Gar was too smart not to know just how strongly he affected her.

She had once vowed never to remarry and never to let a man talk her into bed again. Her first vow had changed as she matured and grew emotionally. Her second vow remained the same. Even as Gar tried to persuade her, she realized that she could never commit her body to an action that wasn't compatible with her own principles.

All she could hope was that she could make him see the folly of his own philosophy. If he didn't, then she would have to stop seeing him, stop talking to him. And that would be the hardest thing she had ever done.

She stiffened her spine. But she could do it if

she had to. All she had to do was remember the past and the horrors of her indiscretion.

She had come a long way from the immature clinging vine she had once been, and she would never repeat those mistakes. She loved Gar with all her heart, but she had to hold on to her self-esteem. That and Marissa were all she had.

CHAPTER FIVE

The young bellboy led Jessica to her hotel room, opening the door with a flourish. She smiled, a slightly puzzled expression on her face as she wondered what she had done to deserve such personal attention.

"Your flowers arrived less than an hour ago." He pointed to the long dresser where a conspicuous floral arrangement of pale pink roses entwined with pale purple irises stood in a crystal vase. The small white card dangled down from the rich incarnadine-colored ribbon, pinned at an angle.

A funny feeling nestled in the pit of her stomach. She knew. Jessica fingered the card without opening it. Still looking at the beautiful bouquet, she asked, "Are you sure you didn't make a mistake?"

"No mistake, ma'am. They were delivered with the instructions that they were to be in your room before you arrived. In fact, there was a telephone call from the party, checking to make sure we had followed his orders." The bellboy looked put out that she could doubt their service.

"Thank you," she said absently before realizing he was patiently waiting for his tip.

After he had gone, Jessica was slowly drawn back to the vase of flowers. He had remembered where she was staying. For reasons she couldn't begin to fathom, a tear trickled down her cheek. He cared. Slowly, with trembling hands, she undid the small pin and opened the card, stalling just in case she was wrong and it was from a store or a dress manufacturer. It wasn't.

> Dinner at seven, don't be late. Missing you like hell until then. Always, Gar

His scrawl looked more like a doctor's prescription than a successful businessman's handwriting, endearing him to her more for that small flaw.

Suddenly the meaning of his note hit her. He was here! He was somewhere in Dallas! Her heart leaped with the joy of knowing he was close. He must have changed his plans and decided he wanted to be with her as much as she wanted to be with him. But a small warning bell went off in her head as she realized the implications of the situation.

Had he decided to come because he still wanted to seduce her, or because he had rethought his stand on marriage? Images of last Saturday revolved through her mind. His kiss had been pure magic—a sultry, sexy magic that she had never felt before. She had been carried away by intense feelings of pure desire unlike anything she had ever known. Joy bubbled inside her, making a teary smile light up her face. He must have felt the same way, no matter what he had said later. He must care. He must! Because she needed him to. . . .

She glanced at her watch. It was a little after five thirty and he would be here at seven. Jessica mentally inventoried her wardrobe, settling on a deep purple dress that would show off one of Gar's roses. It was a soft crepe, ruffled at the collar and cuffs. The very puritanical look of it contradicted itself as it spoke of womanly responsive enticement. Would he understand her message that she was dressing only for him? She hoped so. Her heart careened, her blood pounding through her body as she stared at the woman in the mirror, but saw the man she wanted to be with so badly.

Please, Gar, she pleaded silently with the ghostly form in the mirror. *Please let this mean you've changed your mind on marriage and commitment. Please.*

Gar's eyes almost devoured her. He stood in the doorway, darkly handsome in his navy blue suit, not moving as she smiled up at him, happiness at seeing him apparent in her bright hazel eyes. He could see her nervousness and forced his mind to make his body react naturally, trying valiantly to control his immediate desire. He wanted to take her into the circle of his arms and crush her to him, never letting go. His need for her was almost overpowering. He took a shaky breath and smiled.

"You're beautiful, as usual, Jessica," he finally said.

"Thank you."

His feet wanted to take him directly into her room, but his common sense came to the fore just in time. He had planned this weekend carefully and moving too quickly now could spoil everything.

"Are you ready?"

She nodded and reached for her small silver purse, tilting her head so he could glimpse the soft rose almost hidden in her deep-brown hair. His breath hissed in his throat and he swallowed again. He was thirty-five years old, for God's sake! he admonished himself. He didn't have to act like a teenager in heat.

But his body continued to function on its own,

telling him how much he needed to make love to her.

They walked to the elevator in silence. It wasn't until Gar pushed the button that Jessica finally found her voice.

"I thought you were supposed to be somewhere else this weekend?"

"I never was. I planned to be with you all along. A business associate is taking my calls for me in case of an emergency."

"Why didn't you say something?"

"Because I didn't want you to say no," was his candid answer.

He was right, she thought. She probably would have said no. Yet she couldn't think of anything else she wanted to do more than be with him. His surprising her was what made everything all right. If she had known that he would be there, she would have died from the guilt and finally backed out. This way it was accomplished without all the hassles, and she had nothing to feel guilty about. But she could feel lusciously, delightfully wicked for having a secret tryst with the man she loved.

His hand lightly touched her elbow, sending currents of electricity through her system as he guided her into the empty elevator. The doors silently closed and they descended. The interior seemed to crackle with the mixture of their emotions flowing through the air.

"I hope we reach ground floor soon, Jessica."

His voice was low, growling in a tone that gave away his feelings. "I don't like being this close to you and not holding you against me." His eyes delved into hers, telling her of the intensity of his need better than words ever could. And she responded unconsciously, her body leaning slightly forward as if to touch his, her lips full and slightly pouting as if waiting to be kissed.

The doors whooshed open, and both were brought back to the present. But the memory of their first kiss and the unspoken promise of more to come were in their eyes, hands, and the motions they made while walking across the wide expanse of lobby to the darkened bar hidden in the far corner.

He once more gripped her elbow, pretending to lead her to a small, secluded seat in the corner of the room, but they both knew he needed to touch her as much as she needed his touch.

They ordered drinks, requesting them more to get rid of the cocktail waitress than to have a drink. Jessica didn't need one, her head was spinning with a kind of crazy intoxication already. Just his nearness and her desire for him made her woozy.

"I missed you," she finally said, twirling the drink on the small table in front of them.

"Not half as much as I did," he answered, his voice proving he wasn't teasing. "I missed you like hell but knew if I came on too fast you'd run away. I want you too much to lose you."

There it was—the beginning of his commitment. Her spirits soared. He did care! He did!

She stared straight into his eyes, her love for him there for all to see. "I wouldn't have run," she said softly but with conviction. "I couldn't have. Every time I'm around you, my legs turn to cement." A small wistful smile framed her mouth.

"You do more than that to me," was his husky answer, and she knew just what he was referring to. A light blush complemented her cheeks and she glanced down at her drink, unable to acknowledge the truth that lay between them.

She wanted him, his love, and his body with such a profound force that her body rocked with it.

"Don't look at me like that again, or I won't be able to control myself," he warned her. "We still have dinner to get through, and I'm already trying my damnedest just to keep myself in check. Don't make it impossible for me." His tone was rough, but there was just a hint of pleading that lit her heart with love.

She smiled again and glanced at him through her lashes. "I won't if you won't," she promised teasingly, breaking some of the electrified atmosphere.

"Won't what?" His blue eyes fastened on her mouth, leaning slightly forward, watching it move.

"I won't tease you if you don't tease me."

He finally leaned back, looking relaxed even though Jessica knew better. "I didn't know you were affected by me."

"You're right, I'm not. I always gasp when I breathe," she answered dryly, drawing circles on the table with a long fingernail.

His hand stilled hers, his thumb cupping into her palm to press lightly and cause her to gasp once more.

"I hope I affect you, Jessica. I damn well hope that you're hurting for want of me as much as I am for you. It would only be poetic justice."

They sipped their drinks in silence, his hand still holding hers.

Finally he broke the silence. "I feel like I'm a kid again, sitting in a malt shop and buying a girl a Coke."

"Did you enjoy it then?" she asked.

"No, I hated it. I was always worried that I was going to say the wrong thing and the girl wouldn't let me kiss her good night, let alone do anything else." A chuckle rumbled in his chest.

"And you hate it now?" Her voice showed her disappointment that he would compare her to bad days.

"No, but I still feel that same urge to take my girl in my arms and know I have to wait until we're alone or I'll make a scene." He reached for the rest of the drink and gulped it down impatiently. He couldn't tell her that he had thought

96

he'd seen an end to his days of craving a woman so much, he had to hold himself on a tight leash. Since his marriage he had taken plenty of women to bed, but it had been when he had wanted it and never with such a dramatic intensity of emotions. He hadn't planned a seduction in years. He hadn't needed to. Women today were usually ready, and all he had to do was pick and choose. But not Jessica. For her he had planned and schemed this weekend. Whoever said anticipation was half the fun was crazy. Anticipation was painful and worrisome. What if she had changed her plans, her mind? What if she had said no when he knocked on her door? His mind couldn't cope with the thought.

He shivered, setting his glass down with a thump. "Ready?"

He sounded curt, cold, and Jessica just nodded her head in answer.

Jessica was sure that the dinner was delicious. The restaurant was known for its fine cuisine, so the food must have been excellent. But she didn't taste it. She brought each morsel to her lips automatically; her eyes were fastened on Gar.

She instinctively responded to his every nuance, coming forward when he leaned back, watching him when he spoke, noting his mannerisms. She was filling herself with him and yet wanted more.

She sipped her coffee and cognac, enjoying the feeling of completeness that being with Gar gave

97

her. A glance at her watch told her it was still early. If she were home, she'd be sitting down with the news on television. Perhaps someday she would be sitting in front of the TV with Gar, chuckling at something that had happened at work that day or discussing a piece of news that had just been broadcast. Her thoughts spiraled. They would yawn, both would smile, and they would head for the bedroom, neither really wanting to sleep. Just wanting to be together in each other's arms. Secure. Loving. Needing.

"Where did you go, Jessica?" His leg sidled up to hers under the table and instantly his touch demanded her attention.

"Not too far away," she grinned impishly, refusing to give in to the temptation of placing her hand on his knee to feel the solidness of him.

"Are you ready to go?" His eyes shuttered over; his tone was brisk as he reached for a credit card in his wallet.

She didn't need to answer. He had decided for both of them. It was strange that she didn't mind his autocratic attitude.

She thought he would lead her back to the elevators. Instead, however, he guided her toward another small club where she could hear a combo playing soft, slightly jazzy music.

The room was dark, but Gar seemed to know exactly where he was going as he led her to a corner booth. The cocktail waitress followed them over, placing two napkins in front of them before she wrote down their order. Jessica asked for a light wine, her head already spinning with Gar's intense nearness and the drinks they had had with dinner.

A new song began and Gar reached his hand over the table to her. "Dance?" His eyes held the promise of intimacy. Without thinking, she nodded her head and placed her hand in his as she stood. They walked to the small dance floor, and then he enfolded her in his arms. His hand on her back was like a heated brand of private possession for all to see. Her head was cradled in the curve of his neck, and she could hear the quickening of his heartbeat as her body blended sensuously with his. The beat was slow and elemental, sending a radiating pulse through her system to match it. Their feet barely moved as he held her close, forcing her to feel what she was doing to him and allowing her to know the power she held over his body. She felt heady. Everywhere their clothing touched she became tinted with a fine pale flush. Every time his muscles tensed, Jessica moved in intimate response to feel his reaction and knew his need matched hers.

She felt the feather lightness of his lips as he kissed her brow, and then the viselike grip of his hand as he pulled her hips into a closer, even more familiar contact with his.

Her breath came in short wisps. All the dreams she had dreamed and the thoughts she had thought were now coming true, and her anticipation of his unrestrained touch sent her blood pounding.

"Damn it, Jessica." His whisper in her ear started a pliant reaction in her body. "I was going to take it slow and easy this evening. Now you've got me twisted in knots again."

She chuckled at his admission, not willing to voice the same thoughts herself. She just wanted to float in his arms, letting the world and all its problems fall by the wayside as she stayed sheltered and secure with him.

The music stopped, then almost immediately began again. Gar and Jessica continued to stay where they were, hips slowly moving to the rhythm of the seductive music.

"Jessica?"

She looked up with sleepy-lidded eyes and slightly smiling lips that pouted just a little. She roamed his features possessively, seeing the tautness around his mouth and the slight squint lines around the corners of his eyes. He was tensed, poised, waiting for an answer to his body's question. Slowly her smile disappeared, leaving only a tiny nagging doubt to show in her eyes. Did he care for her enough to know just how much she loved him, or did he just want to go to bed with her? She didn't know and his eyes weren't giving her enough of an answer to judge.

"Let's go." He took her hand, squeezing it until it hurt as he led her to the table to collect her purse before almost marching outside and across the lobby to the waiting elevators.

His jaw jutted in some sort of mental argument or determination as he punched her floor, still holding her hand with a steel grip. He didn't look at her again; he never saw the hurt and confused look that Jessica tried to hide. Apparently he had had enough of her for one evening.

Her heart, just five minutes ago on a string flying high in the air, now plummeted down to earth. He had slowly and expertly primed her body for a night of love, only to withdraw coldly. Every one of Jessica's nerve endings was crying for release from the profound pressure he alone had built up, but no relief was in sight.

Gar snatched the key from her outstretched hand and jammed it into the lock, then opened the door and motioned for her to step in. Jessica did so, then turned slightly, ready to paste a false smile on her lips as she mouthed a hollow but polite thank you, only to almost bump into his chest. He had followed her into the room.

Confused again, she looked up, seeing the stark need in his eyes as he hungrily roamed every part of her body. His hand moved toward her ever so slowly, eating up the inches between them as he reverently touched her waist and hips as if committing them to memory before moving up to cup her breasts in his hands, then traveling farther to the curve of her neck, soothing, smoothing her ragged nerves into another plane of emotions.

"Come here and kiss me, Jessica. Kiss me as if you want me." His hoarse words were an order she obeyed without question.

He was absolutely still, not even blinking his eyes as he watched her come closer. She stood on her tiptoes to wrap her arms around his neck and kiss him on the lips. His breath was released and caught in her throat just as she realized how unyielding he was. But it wasn't because he didn't want her. It was because he wanted her so badly.

Her fingernails trailed through his hair, her lips parting invitingly to seek out his tongue. His slightly clenched hand never left the curve of her neck, but he didn't pull her closer either. He was passive to her touch and she tried harder to arouse his feelings, wanting him to love her as she loved him. She showed him with all her heart and limited experience just how much he made her feel like a true woman.

Finally the dam broke and his arms came around to crush her to his body. She had finally awakened him.

"Oh, Jessica," he breathed when their kiss was completed. "My God, girl, I never thought I'd ever be so lucky to find someone like you." His arms kept her clamped to him. Even the clothing wasn't a barrier to their blatant desires.

"I know," she crooned, soothing the hair she had just ruffled.

He stared at her somberly. "I want you like hell, you know that." She nodded, her heart in her eyes. "But not tonight." He took a deep breath. "Tonight I set out to seduce you, but now I find that I want you to seduce me too."

"Do you think I can? I mean . . ." Suddenly she was flustered. She had no experience to fall back on, not having played the game of love since high school days. She was sad that such a vast portion of her life had been wrapped up in business. Now she doubted her ability to make love to the one she held most dear.

"You can," he chuckled ruefully, "and you will. But not tonight. Tonight I want you to suffer just half as much as you've made me suffer. And I want you to be sure you know what you're doing." His eyes sent her his message, assuring in its sincerity. He cared, and it showed, warming her with his love.

"How long will you be tied up tomorrow?" His voice was a low growl that showed his depth of emotion.

"I'll be through around four."

"Be ready at six thirty. We'll have an early dinner," he promised, before reluctantly releasing her from his hold and forcibly turning away from the softly whispered promises of her body.

Her door was closed quietly but the noise continued to reverberate through the room.

Jessica rubbed her arms where his hands had been, restraining herself from running out in the hallway and calling him back to beg him to make love to her. He was right. She had to have time to know what she was doing, for he was asking for a commitment from her that would last her lifetime. She knew without thinking about it that once she gave him her body, there would be no more denying her love for him. It would be as sacred as any wedding vows for her. And in that giving she would be irrevocably tied to him, whether she wanted it that way or not.

Jessica stepped out on the balcony and sat in the small sling chair that was closest to her. The Dallas city lights twinkled brilliantly, though she didn't see them.

It was a long time before she finally moved from her cramped position and found her way to bed. Her decision had been the same as before.

She would say yes to Garner Pace without reservation.

She loved him.

Jessica and Gar had a quiet dinner Saturday night in a small, quaint Italian restaurant not far from the hotel. They talked of mundane subjects, neither willing to discuss the topic of their growing relationship. It was as if they were testing each other, teasing with words that meant nothing, the intensity of the undercurrent robbing Jessica of most of her coherent thoughts.

Once more her body was tuned to his, her mind filled with his presence. And if his eyes were any indication, he felt the same way. Caresses without touches and nerve endings that sang to each other seemed to fill the air between them.

This time when they walked to her room, she gave him the key without a word.

In equal silence he stared down into the depths of her hazel eyes as if seeking the answer he had wanted. His gaze turned to the key in his hand, weighing it. Then he opened the door and ushered her in.

Jessica placed her purse on the dresser, next to her flowers. She turned slowly to face him, deliberately slipping out of her shoes and slowly walking barefoot toward him.

"Would you like a nightcap?"

His arms opened and she slid into his embrace. "No," he said as he nuzzled her ear. "I want you."

"You have me," she said to his chest, wishing his tie and shirt were off so she could feel his flesh next to hers.

He pulled his head back, looking down at her with a glimmer of doubt in his eyes. "Are you sure, Jessica? This won't be a one-time thing, you know, and once started I don't think I'll be able to let go."

She nodded her head slowly. "I'm sure, Gar. I love you."

A fleeting shadow crossed his face before he slowly smiled. "I know," he stated cryptically. "And I'll love you with all I'm worth."

He turned her slowly in his arms and unzipped her dress, letting it fall to the floor while he pulled her slip over her head to show the beauty of her body. He turned her around, his hands tightening on her shoulders as he filled himself with her presence. Breasts taut and encased teasingly in lace waited for his touch. Slim hips covered with a tiny patch of white silk hugged her skin.

Jessica's hands reached for his shirt buttons, undoing them one by one until she reached his collar. "You'll have to take off your tie. I didn't major in knots in the Girl Scouts," she teased with a husky voice. And he obeyed, shrugging out of his jacket and flinging it in the direction of a nearby chair. She touched his belt, hearing his indrawn breath as she began to free him of his pants.

When they were both naked, Gar took her hand and led her to the king-size bed, pulling down the covers before speaking again.

"Lie down, Jessica. I've imagined you lying in my bed for as long as I've known you. Let reality replace my fantasy."

And she did. There was no reason for shyness in her movements as she rested her head on the pillow and stared up at him with wide hazel eyes. His own deep blue gaze told her of his intense appreciation of the picture she presented. He stood by the edge, watching her legs slowly stretch out, straight and lovely. His heartbeat quickened.

Then he was with her, beside her, covering her flesh with kisses as if she were the drug and he the addict. They blended together in abandonment, each attempting to touch the other's soul with a mind. She stroked the broad stretch of his back, the thick curve of his neck. She clung to him, riding with his ever-spiraling desire as he in turn brushed every pliable curve of her soft body. His hands swept over her now-sensitive skin, only hesitating as he reached the pale inside of her thighs. He waited expectantly and she obeyed his unspoken command by arching her back to him, allowing his intimacy even greater bounds. And he answered by the same method, his hand finding her hidden pulse and bringing it to a greater beat.

His lips teased the curve of her neck. "I knew it. I knew you'd be like this." And before she could answer, his lips covered hers once more.

A bright new world lit with blinding sunshine had opened for her, and Jessica was awed with the force of it. Never in her life had she felt the way Gar was forcing her to feel now. No one had ever touched her as intimately. Not even Thomas, whose teenage fumblings had only resulted in embarrassment for them both.

Her arms encircled his neck and held on as he

lifted his hips to place them intimately over hers. A flicker of concern crossed Jessica's face, as she realized she was unprepared for a night of loving and was unprotected. But Gar sensed her anxiety immediately, and reassured her. "It's all right, darling. I've taken care of everything." Then slowly he came down to fit exactly, giving a warm sigh that brushed her cheek as he settled his weight.

"We were made for each other, Jessica." His lips feathered her temples, his hands soothed back her rich brown hair as he watched the sensuous expressions of love cross her face. And he smiled triumphantly.

With a rhythm set at the dawn of mankind he drew her most erotic nature from her very soul, making her climb peaks she had never climbed before. Breaths mingled as they moaned their responses, each receiving sustenance from the other as they reached the glory of ecstasy.

Their hunger had been appeased for the moment. Gar lay on his back, staring out at the dark night sky through the filter of a sheer curtain, a small smile tugging the corners of his mouth. The room was shrouded in darkness and they seemed enclosed in the safety of a cocoon. Jessica kissed his stomach before resting her head on Gar's navel, her loose hair blending with his lightly haired body, feeling his deep, even breathing and loving the closeness of him.

"Do you know it's three o'clock?" he asked, stroking her dark hair slowly.

"All the better reason to sleep the morning away," she responded, her warm breath teasing his skin. His breathing hesitated before once more continuing, but his heartbeat paced faster, giving an elemental clue to what effect she was having on his system.

One small hand strayed to his hardened nipple, a nail teasing it into protruding. She didn't have to look at his face to know what she was doing to him. A small smile and light chuckle told him of her knowledge.

"It's only three hours till dawn," he growled. "Come here and let me hold you."

Her head came up and she looked at him, seeing the desire in his eyes even in the darkness. "You are holding me."

"The way I want to."

And he did, bringing her up to lie on top and then to the side of him so his hands could roam her curves and feel the softness of her back and softly flaring hips. He gave a satisfied sigh. "You're mine, Jessica," he muttered against her breast. "This is my breast, my hip, my delightfully tantalizing mole. All of you belongs to me."

Her heart warmed. She was amazed at herself for not insisting she was her own person. Gar was the only man she ever wanted to belong to. Her body and her thoughts were his, and she didn't mind at all. She remembered Sheila's words of prophecy, she had seen a pocket full of rainbows in Jessica's future. She smiled. Gar had certainly made sure she had had her share of those.

Then suddenly his hands were doing magical things again, and her thinking stopped as feelings and emotions took over, acting instinctively instead of being told what to do as she completely covered his body with hers.

Once again the lovers' dance had begun.

CHAPTER SIX

The Dallas-Ft. Worth airport was crowded with other weekend passengers as they stepped up to the airline desk, tickets in hand. Gar stood slightly ahead and to the side of her, his three-piece business suit immaculately pressed and tailored. He looked exactly like a handsome businessman should, she thought proudly as she watched with love gleaming in her eyes.

He glanced over his shoulder only to have his sharp blue eyes lock with hers, and she knew he was thinking of the same thing she was—their lovemaking last night and this morning. A warm flush lit her face and she smiled shyly. He placed his briefcase on the ground to hold his place and walked to stand in front of her, leaning down to murmur seductively in her ear.

"If you don't stop looking at me like that, you'll find yourself in some abandoned locker room, making love to a sex maniac."

"Well, I might be agreeable if I knew who the maniac was," she teased back, flirting with him in her happiness.

"I'm the fool, and you know it. There's no one else for you, Jessica. Didn't last night prove that?"

"Oh, yes."

"Just remember it."

Gar's line moved up and he walked back, handing his ticket to the person behind the counter.

Jessica had given him her return flight information this morning, assuming he was going to try to change his so they could be together. There was still so much to discuss concerning their plans for the future. And there had been so little time. She had been loath to bring up such a serious topic in the shining face of the newness of their love for each other.

Gar's hungry eyes devoured her as they finally received their boarding passes and walked to the broad, expansive window of the airport, both ignoring the vast panorama of planes arriving and departing.

Suddenly small lines appeared etched between his brows. His hand reached for hers, holding it between his own with a tight, firm grasp. "Jessica," he muttered in a low, tense voice, then hesitated. Suddenly a chill of premonition flittered through her, flowing down her backbone to land as an ice block in her toes. She waited, knowing and yet not knowing what he was going to say, but realizing that whatever it was, it was not something she wanted to hear. Without realizing it, she slowly began to shake her head, negating the cold tremor that passed through her again.

"Please, no," she muttered through frozen lips, seeing confirmation of his unspoken words in his eyes.

Gar cleared his throat, then began again. "Jessica, remember our conversation in your kitchen last week?"

She slowly nodded her head, mental pictures of his kiss flooding her mind. What did that have to do with his suddenly changed attitude?

He looked slightly relieved, giving her hand a squeeze as if reassuring her. "Good. I was afraid you had forgotten how strongly I feel about Susanna and any other woman in our life."

There it was. The worst had happened. He had put into words what she was afraid he would say. *It was nice knowing you, loving you, sleeping with you, but now it's over.* Only sheer willpower kept her shaking legs from buckling. Only stubborn determination put a tight smile on her lips.

"Are you still afraid of being caught, Garner? Is that it?"

"Yes," he answered honestly. "You're the

113

first person ever to get so close to me in a very long time. It scares me." His grip on her hand tightened even more. But she couldn't see the confusion in his eyes. She was too busy assembling her own reserves into the fore so she could make it through the next hour's plane ride.

Despite the pain, she had to know. If she were to flog herself with past indiscretions, she might as well use the right facts. "What are you saying, exactly?" Was that her voice so calm and controlled? She should have been an actress.

"I'm saying that I want to see you again. Soon. But I want to keep our relationship quiet for a while. I don't want Susanna upset with a situation she thinks will change her life-style."

"You want no demands made on your time or your life, is that it?"

A hand ruffled his hair in agitation. "It's not that, Jessica, it's—"

She interrupted him, taking her hand from his grasp. She stood taller, her hazel eyes blazing with heat and light and sadness and lost dreams. "Excuse me, I'll just go and change my ticket to a later flight."

His hand reached out to grasp her arm before she could leave. "There's no need," he said between clenched teeth. "I'm not on your flight." The confession was forced from him.

Jessica stiffened, not turning to face him. "I see," she said slowly. "This was all thought out beforehand. You knew before you made love to me that you would end our relationship like this. It was all premeditated."

"It's not what you think! I just wanted to assure myself that we didn't get off the same plane and cause gossip. Shreveport is a small city, ripe for gossip and news of any sort. I was only trying to make it easier on both of us."

"You mean for our 'relationship' to continue secretly. Is that it?" Her ankles wobbled in her heels, barely keeping her up, but pride made them stiffen.

"You're taking this all wrong, Jessica. I want us to continue seeing each other. I just don't think we ought to advertise the fact."

Finally she turned to face him, her eyes scanning his face and body as if he were someone she didn't know. "Let's take that one step further, shall we? Let's not see each other ever again. That way there will be nothing to hide. Last week in the kitchen I told you what I was looking for, but you ignored my portion of the conversation as you so wholeheartedly pursued your own goals. I have nothing more to say to you. Now or ever. Do I make myself clear?"

Mercifully, her flight was called. With mist-blinded eyes she fumbled for her gate pass.

"This isn't the end. You know it just as well as I do."

"Oh, yes, it is, Gar. I never want to see you again." A small grimace flitted across her face. "But I do want to thank you for our weekend.

I had forgotten what it was I had missed by not getting involved with a man. Now I know. It's the passion, the guilt, and the heartache. And I can do very well without them."

The plane ride home was a blur. Every two minutes she would stare out only to see Gar's face in the clouds. She would hold back the tears that rushed to her eyes and forcibly change to another imaginary topic in her mind—the new styles she had seen, the orders she had filled out, the shipment dates. Then suddenly Gar would intrude on her thoughts again and the tears would begin pushing at her eyelids once more.

She had wanted to grab his arms and shake him, shouting her love until he finally realized the stark, intimate truth of her words. She wanted him to love her in return. But experience had already shown her that holding on to a person was the one thing that could kill a newborn, adult love. Thomas had shown her that. And in her fear of making the same mistake twice, she had made another. She hadn't told him how deep her love was, hadn't explained that she knew his feelings were based on a heartbreak of his own. She hadn't said the things that should have been said, letting pride and anger get in the way instead.

And now it was too late.

Perhaps not. Perhaps if the next private time

she saw him, she explained, then he would understand.

She silently made a vow to do just that. Surely they would see each other again, if only through the children. Surely he would wait for her to calm down and contact her again, asking to see her. And when he did, she would go and explain her own emotions. She didn't want to tie him to her, but she didn't want to allow time and wasted words to interfere with what could be.

As she exited the plane and crossed the main lobby, Jessica prayed for another chance.

One week from the day she left Gar at the airport, she was still waiting for him to call, to make some sort of overture. But no word came. He had waited outside her house when Susanna occasionally needed to be picked up, but he had never ventured forth or confronted her.

Marissa had finally gone to bed late one Tuesday night and Jessica curled up in the corner of the couch, a brandy in her hand and a velvet robe encasing her body and legs. Ever since she had left Gar standing in the lobby of the Dallas airport, her body had been cold, chilled to goose bumps. An icy rock had settled in the pit of her stomach as she impatiently waited for him to make the next move. Could she be wrong? Did he care for her so little that he would never try to get close to her again?

The phone rang and she jumped before picking up the receiver, grasping it with both hands as she glanced up at the old wooden schoolhouse clock on a nearby wall. It was past eleven o'clock.

"Hello?"

"Hello, Jessica." Gar's voice poured over the telephone wires like warm mercury, freeing her limbs from their chill and heating them to a blush.

She couldn't think of a single thing to say.

"Are you still there?" he asked, concern etching his voice. "Are you all right?"

"I'm fine," she finally croaked, then cleared her throat as she searched her mind for the thousands of words she had rehearsed over and over again. "And how are you?"

"I need to see you."

"Oh?"

"We need to talk."

"About what?"

"You know damn well about what, Jessica," he said impatiently, and she could imagine him on the other end of the line. His masculinity certainly wasn't impaired by the telephone if her pulse beat was anything to go by. As a matter of fact, his voice brought back all the memories she had tried so hard to erase. The thought of his clean-lined body as he left the bed and strolled to the shower, darting a provocative glance over his shoulder at her. His arms holding her tightly next to him, even in sleep . . .

"Damn it! Answer me!" he exploded. "Let me talk to you, explain . . ."

"All right," she answered, and there was a stunned silence on the other end of the phone. She smiled for the first time since last week. Apparently he had not expected her capitulation so quickly. "But if you want to continue with your speech, please, do so. I'd love to hear what you were going to say to persuade me to your way of thinking."

Jessica almost chuckled aloud as the silence continued on the other end of the line. Then she heard Gar's soft laugh.

"Jessica, you're a constant surprise. Perhaps that's the reason I can't think of anything but you and the magic feelings we shared for such a brief time." His voice was laced with regret. He spoke quietly. "Believe me, I've suffered for the past week."

"It's only fair," she admonished softly.

"Are you paying me back? Punishing me for things I didn't do?"

"No, Gar. Only for the things you did do," she answered solemnly. Things like making her love him, need him, want him in her life. The brief intangible things that no one could put a price tag on.

"Will you see me?"

"I said yes. I haven't changed my mind in the past few minutes."

"I'll be right there."

"No!"

But it was too late. He had already hung up. He lived only three blocks away, and if she knew Gar, he would be here in less time than it took ·to brush her hair.

When the soft knock came, Jessica was prepared. She had stood in the center of the room for almost three minutes and mentally outlined what she wanted to say. She had brushed her hair and added a slight blusher to the paleness of her cheeks. And she had answered the door. So far so good.

Once more she curled up in the corner of the couch and he sat in the chair opposite. His hands were clasped between his legs, just like the last time, when they had discussed the girls and makeup. Only this time the topic was them.

"I missed you."

She smiled. "I missed you too."

"Are you still angry with me?"

"I wasn't angry, Gar. I was hurt." She took a deep breath, clasping her hands on her lap. This was the time to tell him. She began quickly, before she could lose her nerve. "You see, I love you. I thought that your coming to Dallas was a way of saying that you loved me too."

His blue eyes closed with her words, as if shutting them out. "I meant what I said that day in your kitchen, Jessica. I'm man enough to want a special woman to share my bed, but I will never marry again. I thought you understood that."

Her heart thumped heavily in her breast. "In other words, what Susanna and Marissa don't see won't hurt them? I disagree. Our having an affair could hurt them far more than a marriage."

His face hardened. "Not if I can help it."

There it was. His intentions remained the same and the only thing that had changed were her own thoughts. She still loved him, but never again would she live with the guilt of completing that love. "You're hypocritical, Gar. It's all right for us to have an affair, but you won't allow our children to know for fear of influencing them. That's no way to raise children. One set of rules for them and one for us."

"They're children and children aren't guided by the same rules as adults."

She groped for the words that would make him understand. They came haltingly. "Once, long ago, I made a mistake and that mistake changed my life. Ever since then I've been cautious about decisions. I know myself now, which is more than I did then, and I know that I can't live with what you're offering." She glanced down at her hands before looking back at him, a glaze of tears in her hazel eyes. "I need a commitment. I need to know that what I do is right, for both myself and Marissa. Rules may change, but morals don't."

Anger flushed his face to a dull red while sparks flew from his blue eyes to heat her own. "And you were so moralistic that you got pregnant in the back seat of a Chevy!" He stood to tower over her, his voice harsh and low. "Excuse me, a Dodge, I think you said! It's all right for some high school goon to make love to you under the guise of love, but you're not mature enough to admit that we had damn good sex together under no guise at all!"

Her words became angry, too, fed by her own hurt feelings. "I never hid the fact from you or Marissa. But I refuse to apologize for it. I made a mistake, Gar, and I learned from it. But you! You made the same mistake, and now you're wallowing in it in your own childish way. You refuse to see that one bad marriage doesn't mean you can't have a good one!"

She stood to face him, not intimidated by his forcefulness.

"Is that a proposal, Mrs. Madison? If so, I don't accept!"

"It wasn't! It was another way of saying good-bye, but you're too thick-headed to realize it!"

"Well, while I'm realizing it, remember this!" His hands grabbed her arms in a steel grip as he pulled her up to him. His lips ground against hers in frightening anger, muffling the sounds trapped in her throat. His tongue rasped against her teeth, forcing her to allow him entrance. She reacted instinctively, without thought of the consequences. Jessica opened her mouth to his invasion only to clamp her teeth closed as soon as his tongue entered.

A low, rumbling growl rent the air as he pushed her away, tears glistening in his eyes from the pain of her bite on his tongue.

"You damn—" Without finishing, he turned and stalked from the room, slamming the front door behind him.

Jessica sat on the couch, where he had thrown her, trembling with reaction to his violence and her own retaliation. What had she done? She could have bitten off his tongue! Only her conscience had come to the fore in time to stop her from drawing blood but not in time to stop the clenching of her teeth.

For the first time in several years, Jessica bawled. Big ugly tears ran down her face to her chin while heaving gasps escaped from deep inside. She lifted the couch pillow to mute the harsh sounds, crying as she had never cried before.

For fifteen years she had secretly believed Prince Charming would come and sweep her off her feet. And when he had finally come, she had chased him off with a bite instead of a kiss. Suddenly it was sadly funny and her sobs turned to laughing hiccups. At the age of almost thirty-two, she had reacted exactly like a teenager in a panic. And so had he.

Somehow that thought didn't help.

"Mom? What's wrong?" Marissa stood in the kitchen doorway, her T-shirt pajama top barely covering her panty line as she peeked over the counter into the den.

Jessica wiped her eyes, shaking her head at the same time. "Nothing, honey. This is just a sad movie," she murmured, not looking up. It had been four weeks since she had been in Dallas and three weeks since the scene with Gar. And she was still having these damn crying jags.

"Sad? Mom, that's a comedy!"

"I know. Something just struck me sad, that's all." She finally had the nerve to glance over her shoulder. "And what are you doing up? You're supposed to be in bed by now."

"I was thirsty." Marissa came around the counter and sat next to her mother, her eyes showing her concern.

Jessica gave her a watery smile. What a beautiful young woman she had grown into. Her dark auburn hair was straight, flowing down her back as if she had just brushed it. Her eyes were full of worry—worry Jessica knew she had to alleviate. But how could she when she didn't have the answers either? She was so frightened herself, she couldn't give succor to her own daughter without explaining things that were best left unsaid. At least for a while.

"I'm just tired, honey. I'll be all right." Jessica

gave a lame excuse, praying that Marissa would let the subject drop.

She didn't. "I don't understand. Ever since you came back from Dallas you've been acting funny. And Susanna said her dad is like a bear! Have we done something wrong that we don't know about?" The young girl's eyes narrowed before widening in comprehension. "Are you angry at Mr. Pace, Mom?"

"No. And my blue funk has nothing to do with you either, unless you've done something you're not telling me about?" Jessica hoped that would ease the subject off her own problems and distract Marissa.

The young girl shrugged her shoulders, not looking directly at her mother. "Nope."

Jessica leaned over and gave her daughter a kiss. "Then go to bed and get some sleep. When you have to get up at five to do your hair, you need all the sleep you can get."

She walked the den carpet long after Marissa was in bed, her body crying out for release in activity as much as her mind called for peace. But neither came.

One question was emblazoned in her mind: Was she pregnant? Had she foolishly, stupidly repeated that most drastic mistake? The thought terrified her, bringing all the harsh, cruel memories to mind of sixteen years ago. All the doubt, terror, and humiliation of the circumstances of her first marriage came back with stinging clarity.

The last time, when she was pregnant with Marissa, she had first denied the truth to herself and others. Then, when she had no choice but to believe it, she had finally told Thomas, only to be jeered at, yelled at, and then barely tolerated by her family and friends. Even her father had understood Thomas's motives better than hers. After all, Thomas had been a boy who was willing to try, but it was her fault for giving in.

She would have laughed at the conversation she had had with Gar just three weeks ago if it weren't so tragic. She had told him to learn from his mistakes but not dwell on them. Perhaps she should have dwelled just a little more.

She stopped in front of the dark living room window and stared out in the direction of Gar's house. She couldn't see it, but she knew he was there.

The only circumstance that was different now was that this time she knew what she had been getting into. A sob caught in her throat. If she had been more experienced, she would have been ready for his loving and protected herself.

She was so stupid!

How could she explain to her own daughter the mistakes of her past and present, and expect Marissa to do any differently? Where did she get off setting up one set of rules for her own child while she lived by another? Isn't that just exactly what she had accused Gar of doing? How could she command respect for her opinions when she didn't deserve it?

Questions kept churning in her mind and she quickly walked back to the telephone, her hand on the receiver, before she finally stopped to think.

She couldn't call Gar.

She couldn't make the same mistake twice. Wanting Gar with all her heart wasn't enough reason to trap him into a marriage that he had already refused.

Her chaotic thoughts traveled the gambit of already tightly strung emotions. Would he give her and her child a name if he thought she was pregnant? Would he grow to hate her as Thomas had, or would he resent the invisible ties that circumstances had bound them with?

Finally, with a sense of inevitability, Jessica made her way through the dark house to her bed. Nothing could be decided tonight. It was best to wait until tomorrow when the light of day would chase away the ghosts of the past, and she would be able to see her predicament in a better light.

One thing was certain. She would put off making any decision about telling anyone until the last moment.

CHAPTER SEVEN

Having finally decided on a somewhat vague course of action, the following morning Jessica found that she could now think of other things. The dress shop had fallen behind in both paperwork and physical labor, but now she was ready to take over again. This was her bread and butter, and if she indeed would have another mouth to feed, then she had better guard her investment. She ignored all other problems even though her own emotional entanglement with Gar remained the same.

Never again, she vowed, would she allow herself to become so involved with a man.

She worked frantically all morning, filled with an impatient energy that awed the salesladies. Clothing had begun arriving as a result of the orders she had written in Dallas, and merchandise needed to be unpacked, pressed, and ticketed for sale. By lunch she was only beginning to slow down to a trot.

"Mary, find more tags for me, will you. I think there are some on the supply shelf," she called out to one of the clerks walking by the shipment door as she rummaged through a box of new sweaters on the floor. "And see if you can order more. By the time this shipment is finished we'll be almost out."

"Right. Oh, and Mrs. Madison? There's someone here to see you." Her voice was sweet, filled with a husky sound that only seemed to be present when a male was around. Jessica's spine stiffened. She knew instinctively who that male was.

He walked into the shipment room, closing the door behind him and leaning against it. "What a beautiful little rump you have, Mrs. Madison." he murmured, his eyes traveling her body and almost physically stamping it with his ownership.

"Get out, Gar. You and I have nothing more to say to each other."

"On the contrary. Common sense seems to desert us at night when we're together, so I thought we could talk better in the cold light of day. This way I can't lose my temper with you for being so obstinate, nor can I make love to you with all these women around. I think it's much better, don't you?"

"And just what do you plan to say that would cause me to be so obstinate you would lose your temper?"

"The truth. That you're only pretending you don't want to see me anymore when we both know that that's what you want more than anything. And so do I." He crossed his arms over his chest, still staring at her as if he'd like to throw her into the box of clothes and make love to her there, in the back room.

She felt a blush attack her cheeks. She couldn't help the blush, but she could stand and face him squarely, which she did. "I don't give a damn what you think. I'm not having any more to do with you. Now, please leave before we both say things that shouldn't be repeated aloud."

"No."

Frustration welled inside her, but she took a deep breath and crossed her arms over her breasts, mimicking his actions. "Then say what you want and leave. I have work to do today."

He didn't move. "Susanna's worried about you, and apparently so is your daughter."

That wasn't what she had expected him to say. She frowned. "Worried? About what?"

"You've been crying a lot lately, sitting up late at night. Not even having an occasional drink with your friends. Susanna says you changed about the same time you returned from Dallas."

"Oh? And does Susanna know why, or is all this on a hunch?"

His face hardened. "It had better be a hunch. I didn't say anything."

"Well, neither did I, Gar. If you think for a minute that I'm proud of what we did, you're wrong." She looked him up and down in disgust, focusing her anger toward him rather than hiding it inside to escape later in the form of tears. "You men! You always go after what you want and are amazed when the female can't handle the stress of such a flimsy relationship! Well, I know my limits, and you're not within the line!"

He walked toward her, his hands dropping to his sides. There was a glow in his eyes, but she couldn't tell from what. Could that have been pain? She doubted it. Gar was too much of a hunter to care whether someone was in his line of fire when he shot.

"Everything that happened wasn't my fault, so don't put all the blame on me. You responded, Jessica, from the very first. Your kisses were blatant in their invitation, your body mine before I ever took it physically. You wanted my hands on your sweet skin weeks before I placed them there. You even helped guide me to you when we finally made love. No woman under protest does that." His voice lowered, velvety as golden brandy as his look seared through her. "But you did."

She trembled from his nearness, frightened yet wanting to touch him one more time. Her hands clenched into small balls. "I made a mistake. A big mistake. I thought we wanted the same thing, but I was wrong."

"You thought I had explained myself so carefully that day in your kitchen only to retract it one week later?" His voice rose on a note of derision, his blue eyes showing his disbelief.

"I know you won't believe it, but yes. I thought you had changed your mind and loved me, wanted something more from our relationship."

"Some love. You only love if you can put a conditional ring on your finger. That's hypocrisy, Jessica."

She couldn't fight him. He was right. How could she possibly have believed that one week had changed his mind? She had known all along that she loved him but he had never professed the same.

"I was wrong," she whispered more to herself than to him. "I was so very wrong." Tears begged to be released, but she held them back through sheer strength of will. She swallowed down the lump in her throat to no avail.

His arms came out and wrapped around her, burying her face in the cashmere softness of his dark gray jacket. One hand came up to clasp her

132

head, soothing her loose hair to her shoulder. She lay against him, afraid to move for fear of loosening the avalanche of tears that were just barely under control. He smelled good, his arms were warm, his heartbeat so very reassuring.

But he didn't love her.

She tried to move away, but Gar's arms tightened. "Stay," he muttered thickly. "Just for a minute. Please."

And she did, wrapping her arms around his waist as an anchor. Quietly she rested in his arms, her eyes closed as she felt the coiled tension slowly seep from her body.

"I do love you, you know." His voice vibrated against her ear. "I just don't believe in marriage as being the solution. It only causes other problems that could be far more devastating."

"I know," she choked into his jacket, lead hitting the bottom of her feet as she realized just how futile their love was. She could never change his mind concerning marriage. Time had healed her wounds, but had only festered Gar's. He would never be ready for a commitment until he realized the past was an error, not a way of life for the future.

"Jessica?"

"Hmmm?"

"Don't turn me away. What we have can continue. There's no reason to end our relationship just because marriage is out of the question."

His words made everything she felt for him

133

seem cheap and tawdry, bringing out into the open what he hoped to keep hidden in the closet. Mistress. Cheap. Lover. A toss in the hay. She could have been picked up in a singles' bar or at a party for all that he cared. A chill ran down her spine. She stiffened.

Gar's hands clamped on her shoulders and he pushed her far enough away to see her face. His answer was there, written in wide hazel eyes in shame and humiliation and fear.

His voice sounded distant. "I see."

She walked to the corner of the room, leaning back against the wall with her eyes closed. She couldn't bear to see his derision, his cold anger. "No, you don't see. I don't want anything from you, Gar. If we had a relationship and our children found out, it would be more my problem than yours. The girls would no doubt understand your biological urges. But they would never forgive me. I don't ever want to see the look in my daughter's eyes that I remember seeing in my mother's when she discovered I was pregnant."

He hesitated briefly, a flicker of something passing over his eyes and then his voice growled like a dark bear's. "Don't be stupid, Jessica. I'd be to blame too."

She laughed through her tears. "And what would you do when Susanna confronts you? Say you changed your mind? I guarantee then you'd forget about having a 'relationship' and I'd be dropped like a clod of dirt. You'd brush your hands of me so fast I wouldn't have time to react."

"Of course not. Our making love was as inevitable as a sunset." He decided to face his doubts head on. "Are you worried about getting pregnant? Is that it? There are other ways of making love, and they're just as enjoyable as—"

She raised her hands to stop his flow of words. "Please! Spare me the clinical details! Since it won't happen again, I suggest you find some other playmate to brighten your day."

"And what will you do?"

"I'll do just fine, thank you."

"Are you still holding out for marriage? Is that it? I told you from the beginning that I wouldn't get married again. I didn't make a secret of that fact, nor did I hold out any other promises except that we would have the thrill of our lives when we finally made love. And we did, Jessica. Some people never have the experience we've had together."

She had finally had enough. Her anger erupted like a string of firecrackers on the Fourth of July. "No! I wouldn't marry anyone, let alone you! I hate you! Can't you understand that I want nothing more to do with you? I don't give a damn whether you exist or not!" She stormed up to him, her eyes turning a deep blue with anger. "Now get out of here before I call the cops! I don't want to see you again!"

His face whitened under her tirade, his fists clenched at his sides to withhold the slaps he felt she deserved.

Jessica left the shop just after Gar's car pulled away from the curb. She needed a quiet place to put her jumbled thoughts in order. But more than that, she craved peace.

Hot tea with a generous amount of sugar cured her trembling hands and quaking insides, but not her mind.

She had lied to him. My God, had she lied! He was right, they had experienced something others never feel. It was her problem that she expected commitment to go hand in hand with their heart-flying experience.

She took a deep breath to brace herself from those thoughts. She had done the right thing. For one fleeting second she had almost pulled him into the whirlpool of marriage. She could have, she knew that. She could have forced him just the way she had been forced years ago. And where would it lead to, except down the path toward a marriage based on lies and misconceptions? No. This time she knew better, and this time she would stand alone.

Gar had primed her for that weekend right from the beginning, never leading her astray from his original intention. It was her own mind that had played tricks on her, allowing her to write a fairy tale with a happy ending when it was really an Aesop's fable with a moral. It had been her fault, not his.

With a sob she suddenly remembered his words in the kitchen over three weeks ago. *I don't want to deceive you, even unintentionally.* He had tried to warn her then, but she had ignored it.

A baby. Gar's baby. She knew instinctively that if she were definitely pregnant, she would carry it, love it, care for it the rest of her life. Marissa would just have to understand.

A strange laugh filled the house before it turned into another sob.

It was dinnertime when the phone rang. Marissa bolted from the table to reach it first, a happy grin splitting her face as she had beaten her mother.

"Hello." Her smile changed to a puzzled frown. "Yes," she answered, then hesitated as she listened. Finally she held the phone toward her mother. "I don't know who it is." Marissa shook her head, the frown still marring her face as she sat back down and tried to pretend she was eating her food, her eyes glued to her mother.

"Hello?"

"Hello, Jessica. This is Thomas. Can you talk?"

"No, not really. Is there something I can help you with? We're in the middle of dinner right now." She clasped the phone tighter, hoping he wouldn't ask her to answer something that would identify him to Marissa. She didn't want to go into any explanations right now.

"Meet me for drinks tonight. I need to talk to you."

"I don't think so. But thanks anyway."

"Wait! Don't hang up. Jessica, please. Just one drink? I promise I'll behave myself. I need to talk to someone. Besides, I need to discuss setting up a trust fund for Marissa."

Her voice hardened, apathy leaving her and anger returning. "Oh, really? How considerate of you after all this time. Are you sure you can afford it?"

"I'll meet you at the Office Lounge in an hour." He didn't bother to answer her question. "Be there or I'll come to the house."

The line clicked off.

"Mom? Who was that?" her daughter asked with a pretense at casual conversation.

"An old friend I met through work. Why?" She lied as glibly as if she had been trained for it.

"No reason. He just sounded slightly familiar, that's all." She tilted her head and looked at her mother, reminding her of a wise old owl. "Besides, I didn't know you knew other men. At least they never called here before."

"He's in town only for a short time. I'm going to meet him for a drink later. Will you be all right by yourself?"

Marissa was instantly offended. "Of course! Good grief! I'm fifteen, Mom! Besides, I need to run to Susanna's for our math assignment, so I'll get it while you're gone."

Jessica grinned at her daughter as she left the kitchen to get ready. Fifteen—if she only realized just how young that was!

Gar walked in the door and threw his coat on the couch before fixing himself a straight Scotch. He downed it in a few gulps and fixed another before finally sitting and forcing himself to relax.

Jessica's words echoed over and over in his head, her expressions flitting through his brain to tease him. He loved her. He knew it and now she knew it. Damn it! Why couldn't she understand how he felt about marriage and accept it?

He could hear Susanna's giggle amid the loud rock music blaring from the stereo upstairs, and knew she was talking on the phone. Probably to Marissa. Those two had hit it off as if they had known each other all their lives. They were more like sisters than friends.

His thoughts reverted back to Jessica.

Ever since he had met Jessica he had wanted her in his arms and in his bed. Intimate thoughts of them making love together had intruded into his very life until he didn't even hear what people were saying to him. His business, which had normally taken up all his waking hours, placed second to thinking of Jessica.

He had engineered the whole courtship ever since their first date. But he had always tried to make her understand that whatever was between them would always remain so without the benefit of marriage. She was a victim of a failed marriage herself and was a sensible business-woman with higher than average intelligence. He had thought she had would have understood that from the beginning.

He took another gulp of his drink. With the exception of Susanna's laughter and the stereo in the background, the house was quiet. Empty. Suddenly, for the first time in his life that he could remember, he was lonely. An aching void in him called out to be filled. Jessica. Jessica.

They had made something very special happen in Dallas. In all of Gar's experience he had never expected the overwhelming response of their bodies and minds that they had given to each other. It was the stuff romances were made of, and he couldn't even begin to explain just how frightening his reactions were. After they made love that first time, he had wanted to leave. Immediately. He knew with a brilliant shaft of insight that he would only become more en-twined with her if he stayed. But stay he did. And the second time they came together was better than the first. When he held her in his arms he knew that he wanted her there for the rest of his life. He needed her. He was afraid to tell her just how much he needed her touch.

But it was more than that. It was her slow-starting smile that lit up her face, and her sensuous walk, and the stimulating conversations they had had. It was the feeling of contentment and peace that invaded his body every time he held her close.

It was love. He loved her more than he had ever dreamed possible. Perhaps that was what made him act so rashly in buying his ticket for a different flight home. He needed to know he could do it, cut himself off from the hold she seemed to have on him.

He flinched thinking of today. He hadn't meant to bring up the fact that he was worried about her getting pregnant, but from the way her face turned white he could tell she had given it some thought and was worried herself. It had just been a shot in the dark, something he hadn't really believed until he saw that look. He had taken precautions, knowing that she wouldn't. She was not the type of woman to be prepared for that type of eventuality. He had realized that, but her closeness had blocked out all sensible thoughts and maybe there was the slightest chance . . . His drink stopped halfway to his mouth; his eyes closed in pain as realization struck him. "Oh, my God!" he muttered, slamming down his glass. He leaned forward, covering his face with his hands. What a damn fool he was!

"Dad?" Susanna stood hesitantly in the doorway, her head cocked.

He slowly raised his head, valiantly attempting to focus his thoughts on his daughter and stop his introspection. "Hi, honey. How's it going?"

"Okay, I guess." She pulled a face as she walked in and slumped into a chair, her leg over the side so she could kick in rhythm to the music upstairs. "Can Marissa come over for a little while, just until her mother comes home?"

Gar tensed. "Sure. Where's Jessica? Working late?"

"No, she's meeting some guy for drinks at the Office Lounge. Strange, isn't it? Marissa said she thinks it's some salesman she met in Dallas. Her mom said it was an old friend, but Marissa didn't think so." Susanna's look was innocent as she watched her father's face turn to stone. "Marissa said it might be serious."

"Marissa said that, did she?" His voice was like hardened leather, stiff and grainy.

"Oh, yes. Of course, that's all right with her. Marissa said she'd like to have a family, you know, with a father and all." Susanna became busy examining her cuticle. "And I can understand. That might be nice."

"You already have a 'father-and-all.'" He grinned tightly, his mind only half on the conversation.

"Oh, I know. But it would be nice to have a

mother or sisters and brothers." She waved her hand in the air. "You know what I mean."

Gar stood up and straightened his tie. "I know exactly what you mean, honey," he said grimly. "I've got some extra work to do tonight. Can you and Mrs. Andrews survive on your own for a while?"

"Sure, no prob. She's gone to the store but should be back soon. I'll call Marissa and tell her it's all right if she comes over." Susanna stood and gave her father a quick kiss on the cheek before leaving the room, a giggle in her eyes. That wasn't half as hard as she had imagined!

Gar's tires screeched down the side streets of Shreveport as he made his way to the bar. He knew exactly where it was; everyone in town did. It was the local watering hole for most of the swingers in town. What could possibly had driven Jessica to go there? Could he have hurt her so much that she would seek love in someone else's arms? No, she was too clear-headed for that. Of course, things weren't that clear right now for either of them. Perhaps he had driven her too far with his no-marriage nonsense.

But it wasn't too late. Now he knew. She belonged to him, and if the only way he could prove it to her was through marriage, then he would marry her.

The parking lot was filled. Gar cruised the block before finally finding a space. He pulled the Cadillac in, cursing under his breath when he bumped the car behind him. There was no time to check now. He glanced at his watch. Jessica had been with this man for about a half hour. His mouth tightened into a thin, grim line. That was all the time that poor sucker was going to get!

He was assailed by smoke and loud music as he pushed open the swinging doors. Gar scanned the crowd, skipping over the many heads that swung his way, a few of the patrons calling greetings to him. He ignored everything in his search. Finally he saw her.

Jessica's head was bent over her drink, tilted sideways and faced toward the wall, as if she were attempting to hear over the din what the man across from her was saying. Gar's glance flickered to the man, noting the blond hair and recognizing him immediately. Surely she wouldn't go back to that rat of an ex-husband! My God! What had he driven her to?

He weaved between the small tables like a slow-moving arrow right on target, his eyes on Jessica all the while. As he got closer he could hear the louder scraps of conversation.

". . . you just don't know! It's like she's trying to smother me with her and the kids. So I moved out. I rented an apartment not far from here." Thomas glanced up to see who was shadowing the table, his open-mouthed expression showing his surprise.

Gar bent down, placing a kiss on Jessica's slightly parted lips. "Hello, darling. I'm sorry I'm late, but the office had a minor problem I had to deal with first." His hand covered hers as he turned to Thomas. He was all charm. "Hello. Tom, isn't it? How are you?"

"It's Thomas," the blond-haired man stated with displeasure. "Look, this is a private conversation between Jessica and me, Pace. Butt out." Bright blue eyes met steel blue and held.

"I'll stay right here, next to Jessica, if you don't mind. And from now on, if you want to see Marissa, make arrangements through me, but you won't see Jessica alone again." He pulled up a chair without breaking his gaze and sat down, his hand covering Jessica's once more. "You had your chance long ago, Madison, and you blew it. She's mine now."

"Jessica," Thomas looked at her, hurt in his eyes as he tried to ignore Garner. "Why didn't you tell me?"

Jessica sat quietly, her heart pounding so loudly she was sure others thought it was the drumbeat of the background music. Her mind had frozen at Gar's entrance, and she still couldn't make sense out of the entire conversation. Gar was going to have Thomas checking through him if he wanted to see Marissa? Suddenly she remembered the lie he had told Artie, then the lie he had made up in front of Thomas. And this was just another one. Only this time

145

she didn't need his help! She didn't need anything from him! She glanced down at her hand and then over to Gar, seeing the softening in his eyes over her confusion. Slowly an anger began to burn in her. Every time she turned around he was lying to someone to get her out of a tight spot. And now here was one more lie.

She tried to pull her hand away, but his grip was tighter than hers.

"Because I didn't know." She smiled, still trying to pull her hand from Gar's.

Thomas looked confused. "How could you not know about your own wedding?" Suddenly his eyes narrowed. "When is the wedding, by the way? I don't see an engagement ring." His eyes watched the two hands on the table and their tug of war.

"Next week," Gar said smoothly, giving her hand a jerk to keep it on the table.

"In a pig's eye," Jessica gritted, jerking back.

Gar smiled. "She wants it sooner, but I said no. I have to clear my desk so we can have plenty of time for a honeymoon. We're going back to Dallas, where we first . . . became entranced with each other."

"Well, well, well. Hello, everyone. Jessica." It couldn't be, but it was. Artie, the man who had been her dinner partner at Sheila's one night, had joined the happy little party. He glanced at Thomas, waiting to be introduced.

Her patience was at a minimum, but if she was

going to salvage the evening, she had to dredge her system for more. "Hello, Artie. This is Thomas Madison and Garner Pace." She couldn't do a proper introduction because Gar still held her hand in a viselike grip. Neither of the men acknowledged the new member of the group. Their eyes were glued to Jessica.

Artie turned to Gar. "How are you doing, Mr. Madison? I must say I never expected to see the two of you in a singles' bar."

Thomas spoke up, his voice unbecomingly nasty and filled with hostile impatience. "I'm Mr. Madison. He's Mr. Pace, and you're not invited."

It was Artie's turn to look confused. "No, he's Mr. Madison. I met him one night when I was taking Jessica home." Thoughts of that night flashed in his head and he quickly decided that that conversation should be dropped. "Well, nice seeing both of you again." He glanced at Jessica's and Gar's hands still attempting a tug of war. Then he looked at the anger on Thomas's face. Finally he looked back down at Jessica. "Life for you is anything but dull, huh, Jessica?" With that he walked away, leaving an even angrier Thomas behind.

"What in the hell was that jackass talking about, Pace? What have you been up to that you've embroiled Jessica in?"

"Nothing that concerns you, Madison." Gar's

voice was not meant to invite any more words, and Thomas gritted his teeth in frustration.

"Jessica, tell this, this . . . caveman to let you go and leave us alone," he ordered imperiously.

"Don't ask a woman to do your work for you, Madison. It's time you left, and to show you that I don't harbor any bad feelings yet, I'll pay for your drink. Now, get the hell out of here."

"Gar!"

"Madison, I'm warning you." Gar ignored Jessica's attempt to interrupt him. "If you want a scene this place will remember for years, you both keep going. If you don't, then Mr. Madison had better leave." He turned away from Thomas, as if he were already gone, dismissed. "And stop fighting me, Jessica. We have enough to discuss without your hysterics." His words were like small pebbles stinging against Jessica's nerves. She immediately stilled. Now she knew why he was the head of a company and Thomas had never made it in the business world. Against her will she admired Gar for taking the situation in hand. And against her will she still loved him.

Jessica watched Thomas stand. He searched her face for confirmation of Gar's feelings, and found them. He gave a shrug and turned away, hesitating only a moment to say "I'll talk to you later, Jessica," before he left quickly.

CHAPTER EIGHT

Jessica didn't bother to watch Thomas leave. The truth was she hadn't wanted to see him at all, but he had given her no choice when she believed Marissa was involved.

She directed her anger at Gar, staring haughtily, waiting for him to speak.

He hesitated a moment, only to stare into her stormy eyes and forget what he was about to say. When his grip relaxed, she quickly slipped her hand off the table and placed it firmly on her lap.

"I . . ." He looked around, suddenly finding the atmosphere suffocating. A flicker of irritation flashed across his face. "Let's get out of here. I don't want to say what I'm going to say in these surroundings." Gar stood, grasping her elbow and leading her toward the door, throwing several bills in the direction of the bartender as they left. She had no choice but to leave with him.

"My car—" she began, but he interrupted her.

"We'll get it in the morning. Right now I want you to ride with me. I'm not letting you go until I say what's on my mind."

"You'd better have something new up your sleeve, to embarrass me like this," she barely choked out, her anger already warring with the seductiveness of his touch. He had loosened his hold on her elbow and was clasping her waist as if she were the finest of crystal. She knew she should move from his side, but despite her anger she didn't want to.

The muffled purr of the car's engine deadened all the street sounds. Keeping his eyes straight ahead, Gar moved through the downtown streets and headed toward the north side and the small expressway. Jessica had a feeling she knew where they were headed, but she refused to question him. Let him wonder what she was thinking.

"It's not working," he said, a smirk in his voice that grated on her nerves.

"What are you talking about?" Her voice was breezy, as if she didn't have a care in the world or a knot in her stomach.

"I may not have known you long, but I know you well, Jessica. You think silence will freeze me out. But it won't. I won't allow you to put a barrier between us. Not anymore." He turned into the parking lot of a large six-storied building of chrome and glass. This was the headquarters for Can-Do-It stores. Gar's company.

It took all of three minutes for them to reach his set of plush offices from the entrance of the building. A large, well-lit elevator rushed them to the top, where they walked a wide hall directly into his secretary's office, then into his.

One wall of glass faced the west, allowing her to imagine the scene a spectacular sunset would create. It would fill the entire room with its colors. The rest of the office was decorated in golden tan and rust, beautifully executed by a skillful professional.

Gar walked her over to the low, cushioned couch, making sure she was seated before walking to the desk and sitting on the edge of it. His pants tightened to mold to his skin as his legs stiffened to prop him up.

He stared at her, his blue eyes roaming her face and form as if he were seeing her for the first time. His expression softened, a smile turning up his sensuous lower lip. She watched in fascination as she saw the change and her heart tugged unwillingly within her breast. What had happened to make this man the one who could turn her into a puddle of rippling warm water? Why just this man?

"You're pregnant with my child, aren't you?" His voice was molten lead, soft and heavy.

It took a minute for the words to be absorbed. When they did, she turned her head and stared out the dark window. Her face was stiff and white with guilt, but she wouldn't let him see. Now was her chance. She could tell him yes and he might feel obligated to marry her. But she knew that he wasn't ready for the emotional commitment she needed from him. He was still fearing marriage, still healing from the burning he had received the last time. What could a marriage based on forced issues be like under those circumstances? She knew the answer. Disaster. Just like it had been with Thomas. Granted, they weren't anything similar in personality or traits, but the circumstances were the same.

"Whether I am or not is no business of yours," she answered quietly, knowing her choice had been made.

"It certainly is. I want to marry you, give our child a name. My name."

She still kept her face averted. "Really? Why would you do that?" Slowly she faced him, her eyes distantly curious yet not concerned. She was hiding inside herself so the pain of his words wouldn't catch her off-guard and pierce her own invisible armor.

He could feel her total withdrawal and clenched his hands to keep from shaking her into a reaction, any reaction. "Because the baby is my responsibility too."

"Oh, like you're responsible for Susanna, your

business, your cars? And what kind of a marriage would we have, Gar? Would it be a good one because this is what we want, child or no child? Or would the resentment of being trapped build inside of you? Would you wind up hating me, and hating yourself for being so careless?"

Silence answered her. His mouth formed a thin line; his dark-blue eyes iced over. She had her answer.

Jessica stood. She strived to make her voice as calm and controlled as she could, shoving the lump in her throat down to the pit of her stomach. "Thank you for the kind and generous offer, but my answer is no, thank you."

"Sit down." His voice was low but edged with frustration and impatience.

"No. I think we've had this conversation before. I don't want you, your hand in marriage, or anything else. Now do you take me home, or do I call a cab?" She stood facing him, her chin lifted in determination. She didn't care what he thought of her, she had to get out of here.

He walked to stand in front of her, his hands itching to squeeze her pretty throat. Instead, they curved to her waist, bringing her into closer contact with him. She could feel the strength of his thighs, the intimacy of his hands, as his fingers splayed to touch her ribs and the undersides of her breasts.

"You and I have something too precious to just throw it away because of pride. We both know that," he growled, his face burying into the arched side of her slender neck. "Don't do this to us, Jessica."

"Are you saying that you really want to marry again?" Her voice sounded husky even to her own ears. She tried to keep a firm hold on her sanity, but his teasing mouth was making that hold a tenuous thing at best.

"I'm saying I don't want to let you go." His lips moved from the softness of her cheek to her slightly parted mouth, breathing her breath, touching her skin, feeling her form. A shiver went through his body and transmitted electrically to hers, forging them together in a heated embrace. One hand came up to cup her head and move it with his so their bodies could blend even closer.

So intensely involved with their lovemaking, they sank to the couch without Jessica's realizing it. One by one, Gar's shaking hand undid the buttons of her blouse. Then with a quick snap, her bra was undone and her silken breasts sprang free to his wandering hands. His lips continued to play teasingly with hers while his touch ignited a radiating candescence through her veins. Slowly his lips left hers to seek sustenance elsewhere—the hollow of her throat, the deep cleavage between her breasts, and finally to one dusky-hued peak. He circled the aureole with his tongue, teasing it rigid, enjoying her quickened breath and slight sighs as she silently begged for more. She arched her back, a moan leaving her lips as he finally captured the taut nipple and lavished it with his silently active praise.

Her hands moved through his dark hair, loving the texture and feel of it. They traveled down the strength of his neck to his slightly hunched back, feeling the muscles move and ripple. His arms were braced and rigid, holding the bulk of his chest weight so he could better reach the fulfillment he craved.

The room was filled with whispered sighs, the hands with texture and tones of unyielding flesh. The movements were slow and easy as they reveled in the heady contact of each other. Their bodies melded and blended as if the inner clock of time told them how to weave such an intricate pattern of shoulders and torsos together without losing contact of flesh upon flesh and breath mingling with breath.

He took her hand and led her to his belt, miming his instructions to her as he continued to ply her with kisses and caresses, and she obeyed until the zipper was down and she could feel the heat of him next to the coolness of her hand.

"I was right, Jessica," he whispered in her ear. "We're so good together." His hand crept up the inner softness of her thighs, his rough skin teasing her nerve endings into a heightened anticipation of his more intimate touch. She knew where he would go and she longed for him to bring her to exploding release. A warm dampness invaded her, stunning her with its impact. She knew what it was immediately and her mind blinded itself to his next words, she was so wrapped in her own thoughts.

"You can't forget me any more than I can purge you from my system."

All her nerves twisted and created a numbness, chilling her system that had been so overheated just seconds earlier. Gar stared at her, believing his words had turned a magic switch and the power was shut off. As quickly as she became chilled, he stilled, realizing at once that he should have kept his counsel, and cursing his own inability to do so.

She didn't say a word, but her body screamed, *Let me go.* He answered by withdrawing, standing, shoving his shirt back into his pants, and buckling his belt. He stared down at her, his eyes never leaving her face as she gazed steadily at the ceiling.

She heard the zipper being pulled and locked.

She heard him walk away, back to the edge of the desk.

She continued to stare at the ceiling.

"Cover yourself," he rasped. "Unless this is part of the punishment you seem to want to put me through."

She drew her blouse over her still-loose bra,

not moving from her prone position on the couch.

"Sit up."

Her obedience was his frustration. He ground his teeth as he watched her do as she was told. Now, instead of looking at the ceiling, her eyes were locked with the floor.

"Tomorrow, after a business meeting, you and I are going to get a marriage license. We'll be married quietly, at home, with just the children and a few close friends in attendance."

Slowly her head rose until her eyes, cold and detached, met his. "No."

His blue eyes, equally cold, held and clashed with hers. "Yes."

Jessica took a deep breath and let it out slowly. "I've told you things about myself that I've never told another person. I even told you of my big mistake in life; one I believe I've paid for a thousand times over in a million different ways. I will not make the same mistake again. Not with you." He began to interrupt, but she raised her hand and continued. "It took me this long to recover from a marriage doomed from the start. You haven't gotten over yours yet. It would be a disaster."

"I'm not giving you a choice."

"You're wrong. I'm not giving you one. I am not pregnant."

Her words hung like dust motes in the air,

settling softly only after the breeze of her words had ended.

His jaws clenched together as if in pain. His hand came down hard on the solid surface of the desk. "You're lying!"

"No." Her head went from side to side, proof of her conviction showing in the depth of her wide hazel eyes.

"I couldn't have been wrong! When I mentioned pregnancy in your shop, you turned pale at the thought. Was that just a reaction to the past?" He pushed himself away from the desk and hunched down in front of her, his hand automatically sweeping her hair away from her face with tender hands. "Tell me, Jessica. Talk to me," he pleaded in a rough voice, sensing the conflict of emotions she was experiencing, yet not knowing the cause.

"I was afraid of pregnancy then. I'm not now," she finally answered. Before he could say or do any more, Jessica moved away from him. "Please, Gar. Take me home." Her voice was weary, tired.

And he wordlessly complied, knowing he would have another day to change her mind.

By the time Jessica reached home, Marissa was in bed and the house was very obviously quiet. She reached for the stereo and played some slow, easy music before taking a quick shower and crawling into her favorite place on the couch to sit and stare into the unlit fireplace, a glass of white wine in her hand.

She was an empty jug and depression was the dark water that filled her. She didn't understand it, but she had been depressed when she thought she was pregnant. And yet, this morning, when proof finally came that she wasn't pregnant, she was even more depressed. Some would probably say that the reason she had thought she was pregnant was because she was so afraid of being so. Or was it that she had wished she were? She didn't know. She wasn't sure of anything anymore.

She shook herself to rid her mind of the thoughts of what could have been. She had made the right decision in telling Garner the truth. She knew it. But it didn't seem to make her feel any better. She had lost him. Disjointed thoughts flitted through her mind. Thoughts of him in the kitchen, kissing her. Gar sitting in the chair across from her, asking her to stay out of his daughter's life. She remembered a different Gar in Dallas—carefree, fun, sexy, and loving. Oh, so loving. He had cared, she knew it. But not enough to bury the skeleton of a past marriage and begin a new life with her.

He hadn't healed his wounds from the past. It was as simple as that. And she couldn't continue a relationship that wasn't based on honesty and trust. To do so would be to forget everything she had learned in all those years. It would slowly tear her apart and leave her bleeding from the wounds again, not to mention the effect it would have on the children and their relationship.

Tears slowly paved a way down her cheeks to plop on her robe. She didn't cry aloud or sob, just silently let them fall as she took out each memory to examine it before burying them in the dark subconscious of her mind. Tomorrow would be soon enough to forget, but tonight was for grieving.

"Take the new shipment to the back and see what needs pressing, Mary." Jessica walked toward the counter, her head bent over the invoices. "I'm going to see if I can make head or tail out of this invoicing." She shoved her hair back with an impatient hand, only to have it fall along the side of her face again.

"Yes, ma'am." Mary exaggerated a curtsey before wheeling the dolly to the back of the store. Her sarcasm went unnoticed by her boss.

"Hi, Mom! What's up? Anything new in today?" Marissa and Susanna breezed in the door, both in jeans and rock group T-shirts and looking for all the world like day and night even though their clothes matched. Susanna towered over Marissa by at least a full head and her shoulder-length blond hair was carelessly piled up to make her seem even taller. Marissa's curly dark hair tossed around her shoulders, her small body dwarfed by Susanna. Yet they both were striking in different ways.

Jessica gave a half smile, forcing herself to look pleasant. "Hi, girls. There're new sweaters in the back room if you want to help Mary unpack them," she said.

Susanna gave a giggle and turned to the back of the store, eager to see the contents of the boxes that had just arrived. Marissa hovered around the counter.

The invoice numbers weren't corresponding to the order blank Jessica had fished out of the file. "Damn," she muttered under her breath.

"What's the matter, Mom?"

"What?" Jessica glanced up, surprised that Marissa was still there.

"I said what's the matter?" Marissa mouthed her words slowly, as if her mother were reading her lips. "You've been in a bad mood for two weeks now." A frown creased her brow. "Is it Susanna? Don't you like her?"

"Of course I do," Jessica assured with a shaky smile. "I've just got other things on my mind." She wouldn't admit for the world that Susanna reminded her painfully of Gar. She wouldn't even admit to herself that Gar was still in her thoughts both day and night.

"Are you sure? I know about you and Mr. Pace seeing each other—" She broke off when she saw the pained look on her mother's face.

Jessica didn't seem to hear her daughter's

comments. "Go with Susanna and look at the sweaters, would you? I need to set this problem straight." Jessica turned unseeing eyes back to the papers in front of her. There was no need to do more than look busy. Besides, her mind wasn't functioning anyway. She just needed some time to pull herself together . . . again.

Marissa walked away silently.

Jessica continued to stare at the papers on the counter.

Neither would openly admit the change of character roles in their lives. Marissa was now worrying like a mother and Jessica was now acting confused and troubled, just like a teenager.

The sophisticated dark-haired woman across from Gar smiled invitingly at him, her hand squeezing his knee under cover of the elegant tablecloth. "Honey, I'm not asking you to spend the rest of the night with me, just an evening of fun and games will do." She chuckled throatily.

Garner smiled knowingly in return. "Am I supposed to disappear at midnight, Michelle, like a pumpkin, so you can get your beauty rest?"

"You never used to mind," she retorted huskily. "You used to say I was worth it. What's the matter? What's changed you so much since the last time I saw you? We used to have so much fun."

162

"Nothing's changed." He barely kept his words from snapping. "I haven't seen you in three months. Perhaps your imagination is working overtime on 'what used to be.' I'm the same."

She shook her perfectly coiffed head. "No, something's different," she quietly insisted. "I'd bet my latest diamond that it has to do with another woman."

Her jab hit home. His insides flinched. "Not all your diamonds?" he tried to tease, wishing he could think of some way to change the subject, but his mind wasn't working at its usual fast pace lately.

She smiled once more. "No, honey. I never lay it all on the line. That's sheer foolishness."

When he didn't spar in return, Michelle sipped her wine and watched him, her guessing eyes wide in speculation. "How's Susanna?"

"Fine. She wants to grow up too fast. Some fresh kid asked her out for a date tonight, but I told him to come back in two or three years. Fifteen is too young." His eyes stared slightly over his date's shoulder as he remembered how crushed Susanna had been. She had run to her room, crying, but his consoling hadn't helped matters, it had only made the situation worse. Even Mrs. Andrews had been miffed with him. Damn it! Was he the only one who saw the real dangers of dating too young?

"And I bet you handled that well, using a

sledgehammer to nail a tack in the wall," Michelle answered dryly.

He focused once more on her. "And how would you have handled it?"

Her well-manicured hands went up in the air. "Don't ask me, darling. I don't have children, don't want them, and can't remember anything more dull than my youth. You're the papa. What you need is a younger woman for a housekeeper. Someone Susanna can relate to and who can help you with all those girlish problems." She leaned forward, whispering conspiratorially. "I handle the big boy's problems."

The waiter brought white china plates of prime ribs and rack of lamb, setting it before them with a flourish. Gar leaned back and watched Michelle begin her meal. She ate like she made love, with all her attention focused on the moment.

Suddenly he felt alone and wished he were home. He had played this part for ten years—the merry bachelor priming the already-willing woman before taking her home and joining her in her bed. It had always been a game, a lark, and suddenly it was not enough.

A vision of auburn-flecked hair spread on a white pillowcase and wide hazel eyes staring at him with contented love flitted through his mind, leaving a searing pain in the middle of his stomach. A longing he had hidden so well in the past two weeks flooded through him.

He was disgusted with himself for being here when this wasn't what he wanted, and he had known it when he had called Michelle. He craved the peace and sweet contentment of other arms, the almost unbearable, tantalizing ecstasy of another body. He wanted Jessica so much that it hurt to pick up his glass.

He tried to reinforce his past actions by remembering the lesson he had learned so well from Carla. She had trapped him into marriage by getting pregnant, then trapped him into fatherhood by leaving him with Susanna. Shouldn't that have been lesson enough for any man?

Suddenly Carla didn't seem important anymore.

He'd been a fool!

He leaned forward. "Michelle, I wonder if you'd mind doing me a very big favor. . . ."

CHAPTER NINE

"Sheila, if I wanted a date, I could have one. I just don't feel like going out." Jessica tried hard to keep her voice even, but her irritation leaked through, giving her best friend the opportunity to make a sad, hurt face.

"But after I explained it all to Arnie, he really wants to take you out again. He's promised he'll behave himself and let you set the pace," she said sweetly, as if they hadn't been arguing about this over coffee for the past fifteen minutes. "Don't you think you owe him just one perfectly harmless date after that fiasco you put him through at the Office Lounge? He was trying to do business with Garner Pace and now feels that he'll never get an appointment to see him, and all because of that episode."

"But why me?" Jessica tried to find other excuses to keep her from doing what she knew Sheila would eventually wear her down into doing. "Arnie isn't a bad-looking man. He must know hundreds of other women more than willing to have dinner in a nice restaurant and meet his boss from Ohio. Dozens of single girls come in the shop every day, and they're all searching for a man to treat them to a night on the town!"

"He doesn't want some silly secretary who's looking for a nice husband wrapped in a neat package. He doesn't want to get involved yet either." Sheila sipped her coffee, looking over the rim to see how her words were affecting Jessica. She didn't know the reason why, but Arnie had begged her to have this talk with her friend. And Jessica looked as if she needed a night out, away from the pressures of business and home. She was pale and had lost weight. Her listlessness was obvious in just the way she sat there with Sheila, and Sheila didn't like it. All the sparkle had left Jessica's hazel eyes. "He's looking for someone presentable and safe, and you're it. He just wants a girl for the occasion, not to get married to again. And, besides, he doesn't have all the time in the world. He only has till this Saturday."

"Since this is Friday, I suggest that he get a move on," Jessica said dryly, still obstinate in her stand.

"All right," Sheila said carelessly. "I'll tell

him no go. It's no skin off my nose if you stick around the house looking like the last of an old moon. If you don't care what people think, why should I?" Her face was innocent of all expression. Only her eyes gave away the fact that she was more knowledgeable than she was admitting.

Jessica leaned back in her seat and threw her arms in the air. "I give up! I give up! You've sold me on the merits of having a platonic date with an octopus!" she exclaimed, smiling. "You really ought to sell funeral insurance. You'd make lots of people buy even when they know they won't give a darn when the time comes!"

Sheila bowed her head in acknowledgment. "Thank you. I'll take that as a compliment."

"Whether it was or not," Jessica muttered in reproach, but she couldn't keep the smile from her eyes as she said so.

Marissa stretched across the bed, her head in her hands as she watched her mother lightly apply her makeup. "And you really want to date this guy?"

"I'm doing it as a favor," Jessica informed Marissa, her eyes on the eyeliner pencil.

"Some favor," Marissa snorted, rolling over. "But try to have a good time anyway."

Jessica laid down the pencil and turned to her daughter, hesitating to bring up what she was about to say. "Marissa? You don't mind that I'm dating, do you?"

"No. Why?" Marissa raised her hips and legs off the bed and began doing a bicycle exercise.

"No reason. I was just wondering if you resented it, that's all."

"Because of Dad?"

"Well, yes."

"I know lots of girls without dads, Mom, and they're doing fine. Besides, I don't even know my father. I remember him, but my not knowing him now is his loss!" She grinned, successfully covering up the hurt feelings that washed over her when she thought of how expendable she must be. But with self-confidence born from her environment, she shrugged it off.

Jessica took a deep breath. No time like now to plunge in. "Your father called me at work last week. He was sorry he couldn't see you, but he's been transferred to Kansas City. He'll be living there from now on."

"Gee, I'd hate to be living with him and have to change schools right now," was the only comment Marissa made.

"His family is still here, dear. Your father is getting a divorce." Jessica watched in the mirror as Marissa digested that bit of news.

Her eyes locked with her mother's in the mirror, a deep, thoughtful look in her eyes. "Someday I'd like to have a new father, someone like, oh, I don't know, like, Mr. Pace, maybe. And I'd like to have brothers and sisters. But I'm not childish enough to feel resentment because I can't have what I want." Marissa brought her feet down with a thud, rolling over as she once more looked at her mother.

Jessica could feel the flood of a blush at Marissa's words and turned to face the mirror once more.

"I thought you considered Mr. Pace too strict," she finally said.

"He is, but you could loosen him up."

A pain of remembrance shot through Jessica as she remembered their last encounter. "No. Not me, darling. You'll just have to survive your teenage years with me unmarried."

"Okay, Mom." Marissa slipped off the bed and leisurely sauntered out of the room.

Jessica stared at the woman in the mirror only to see Garner as he looked when he had leaned against the desktop. She loved him. He loved his freedom from a binding love. That was a difference of opinion that could never be reconciled. It was better to forget him than to have the thought of what could have been haunt her for the rest of her life.

Suddenly she felt old and used, and most of all unloved. What was the matter with her? She remembered reading somewhere that the biggest mistake in second marriages was the fact that the woman always chose the same type of man. Had she been any different? Yes, a voice answered. She had fallen in love with a man who was honest and forthright. He had told her from the beginning just how things were and she had refused to accept that.

It had been her fault. But she had redeemed herself when she had refused his proposal.

A sudden flash of insight almost blinded her.

He had proposed! All along he had said that he would never repeat the same mistake he had once made before. Yet, when he thought she had been pregnant, he had proposed! Did that mean that he really did care as much as he said? Or was everything a pack of lies? No, he wouldn't have stated either if that were the case. Her spirits declined as quickly as they had soared. He did care; it just wasn't enough to marry without being pressured into it. And she couldn't accept those circumstances.

Jessica stood and straightened the small belt on her silver-gray dress. It was over. That was it. There was no use thinking of Garner Pace anymore.

She kept telling herself that with time the wounds she felt would heal. She could only hope so, but reality was different from wishing.

"You look great, Jessica," Arnie said, a small corsage in his hand.

Jessica smiled. He looked like a high school boy taking his girl to a prom. "Thank you, Arnie. I'm ready if you are. I'll put your flowers on just before we reach the party. I don't want them to get crushed."

A guilty look passed over his face. "I forgot to mention that I'm taking you out to dinner first. I thought we could enjoy the beginning of the evening together, then go to the boss's house."

"Oh? Isn't the party beginning soon?" she asked, not really concerned one way or the other. It was just a way to spend an evening.

"Not until nine or so," he muttered, closing the door behind her and holding out his hand for the key.

"That's fine."

The restaurant was crowded but he had made reservations and they were led to their table immediately. The atmosphere was quietly restrained, the service impeccable.

Jessica relaxed in her chair, her eyes darting around the room but not really seeing anything. She wasn't interested in how many women were wearing her dresses. She just didn't give a damn.

Arnie rambled on about the lumber business. Jessica nodded at all the appropriate places, making a soothing sound when needed. She wished she hadn't been talked into this date, for her head was fuzzy and she lacked the interest necessary to carry on her end of an intelligent conversation. She would have been far more comfortable curled up on the corner of the couch reading a book.

Her neck itched. She ruffled her hair back, soothing her skin with the palm of her hand, but her neck still itched. She stiffened. Turning slowly, she once more scanned the room of people, forgetting that Arnie was talking to her, forgetting everything when she saw that Gar was sitting two tables away from her, his eyes watching every move she made.

And he wasn't alone.

A beautiful brunette was seated across from him, her dark upswept hair showing off her bone structure and haute couture. Jealousy stabbed through her body, hitting every nerve with a jolt. Jessica lowered her eyes, unable to bear having him see the pain there as she swung around to face Arnie once more. Her lips trembled; her heartbeat raced in her breast. Her mind went blank of things to say or do. All she was aware of was Garner's blue eyes drilling through the back of her head.

Jessica grabbed her wineglass and took a big gulp to push away the lump in her throat. She wanted to hide, move, get out of there. Anything.

"Jessica? Are you all right?" Arnie leaned forward, his concern showing in his face.

She glanced up, her mind a daze. "What?"

Arnie's gaze slid from her to Garner and then back again, turning into a grimace as he did so. "So it's true, your feelings for Mr. Pace," he muttered.

Before she could answer, she felt Garner's presence at her side. "Good evening, Jessica, Arnie." He nodded toward the other man but his piercing eyes never strayed from Jessica's downbent head.

"Good evening, Mr. Pace. I trust the food was good?" Arnie said, and Jessica looked up then, the tone of his voice telling her he had spoken and made peace with Gar since that episode at the Office Lounge. But, how, where, and why?

"As good as you said it was," he clipped. "Jessica? Are you through eating now?"

Pride made her finally raise her head to stare at him. She couldn't ignore him as she'd like to without causing a scene in a restaurant already filled with avid listeners.

"Why?"

He reached for her elbow and pulled her up. "Because the band is playing our song."

She marched beside him to the small parquet floor in the next room, numbness still surrounding her. There was no way she could refuse without calling attention to them, and that she had no intention of doing. She would be as cool as she could be, never letting on her feelings and hoping her body would lie. But when he folded her in his arms, she suddenly came alive again.

"How dare you humiliate me like this," she whispered angrily, vying for more space between them. She still couldn't leave him without making a scene, but she certainly didn't have to touch every part of his body. "This town is too small for your kind of behavior, Gar." She narrowed her eyes. "Or is that it? Are you trying to punish me for turning down your original generous offer of being a hole-in-the-wall mistress? Is this your way of getting even?"

"I don't give a damn what anyone thinks, Jessica, so be still and let me hold you close to me for a while or I'll make an even bigger scene." He spoke into her ear as his grip around her waist tightened, bringing her into closer, more intimate contact with him.

They took several dance steps before she could find the voice to speak again. She had to break the spell he was weaving around her. "Don't you think your date will mind your leaving her all alone?"

"I don't know. Would you?"

"Yes. I'd scratch the other woman's eyes out," she said before she realized what she was saying was giving away her innermost feelings.

A chuckle rumbled deep in his chest. "I'm almost tempted to see that."

"Don't worry. I'd only do it with someone else. You're not worth fighting over." She hoped her jab hit home, but it didn't seem to affect him in the least.

"Yes, I am, and you know it," he answered smugly. "So behave yourself. I don't want to fight with you right now. I want to feel your soft

175

body next to mine as you undulate those neatly packaged hips to the music."

Jessica quieted in his arms. No matter that he wanted to feel her body. She wanted to feel him too. Her hand clenched at his broad shoulder and her head rested against his throat. This could well be the last time they were together and she might as well enjoy it. Slowly, almost reluctantly, the music came to a halt. Her heart thumped in her breast at the thought of parting from him, but she knew she had no choice. It was either that or—suddenly the meager amount of love he had to offer seemed better than not having him at all. For one crazy moment she wanted to shout at him, berate him for asking her to have an affair and keep it a secret. Then she wanted to accept him on his terms. Anything rather than let him go. A life without him was too miserable to contemplate.

"Stay right here; don't move," Garner muttered, giving her a quick squeeze before abruptly leaving her embrace. She stood in the center of the dance floor by herself, suddenly feeling foolish and alone.

Without a thought given to Arnie, she quickly turned and walked toward the door. She'd get a taxi and pay him when she reached the house, but she had to get out of here.

A hand grasped her waist before she had even made it to the outside door.

"I thought I'd told you to wait?" came the voice from directly behind her, and she turned.

Her hazel eyes were blue with unshed tears that threatened to spill any minute. "No, Gar, please. I can't take any more. Please, leave me alone," she pleaded, a lump once more growing in her throat. She was supposed to have pride. What was the matter with her, begging like this?

"Hold on to your purse, honey. You're coming with me," he muttered into her ear as he pushed the outer door open and led her through, a firm grip on her arm guiding her toward his car.

"What about Arnie? Where's your date?" she babbled, saying anything that would distract her from what she was doing. She tried to hold back, her feet stumbling as they walked.

"You didn't worry about Arnie when you walked off the dance floor. Why now?"

"I didn't think, that's why! Every time you're around I seem to make a great big fool of myself, but not anymore, Garner Pace! Let me go! I came with someone, I'll leave with the same man!"

"No, you won't." He opened the side of the Cadillac and almost pushed her in. "Arnie is happily occupied with Michelle, finishing a free meal with a woman who will soothe his ego instead of giving him romantic ideas."

He walked around the front of the car and

slipped into the driver's seat, starting the engine quickly and taking off.

Jessica sat rigid, her hands clamped together in her lap. "Why are you doing this to me, to both of us?" she finally questioned quietly, her voice barely breaking with the strain of their being together. "What do you hope to gain?"

"You."

Jessica took a deep breath and slowly exhaled. She continued to stare out the window, unable to face Gar as she said what she knew had to be discussed. "All right. You have me. I'll be your bed partner and I won't tell anyone. I'll try to be discreet."

The car slowed to a halt in the middle of the street as Gar turned to stare at her. "What?" He sounded stunned, even to Jessica's ears.

"I said, you don't have to go through with this . . . this sham of caring. I'll be what you want."

The car sped up, passing the telephone poles on the side of the road and making them a blur. "Why?" he asked curiously. "A change of heart? Have you decided you can do without the public brands of marriage and togetherness?"

"No," she answered slowly. "I find that I don't do very well without you. I love you, Gar. I don't want to be without you. Maybe, with time, you'll find that you've healed those wounds that make you so afraid to commit yourself. I want to be there when it happens."

178

"And if it doesn't happen? What then?" His voice was ragged, his breathing light.

"Then at least I took the gamble and tried." She gave a careless shrug, knowing he couldn't see the tears that threatened to run down her cheeks.

"Why would you do that? Take such a chance?"

"I told you. I love you."

"But I've already said that to you."

"Yes, but you've never recovered from your first marriage. A marriage, good or bad, is always with you—it shapes your life. Especially one that ends with heartache and failure. I've finally reached the stage where I realize that I cannot change the past, but I can change the future. Although you haven't recovered yet, I see the symptoms of recovery, and I'm willing to bet that someday you'll want another commitment and I want to be there when that happens."

A moan seemed to issue from his lips. It was a low, torturous sound that flooded her entire body with compassion for him. She knew she was taking a big chance, that he could leave her cold and lonelier than she had ever been before, but what choice did she have?

He pulled into the driveway of his home, impatiently flicking the power-door opener and driving into the darkness of the garage. The motorized door smoothly shut behind them. He turned off the ignition and lights and sat, staring straight ahead for a silent moment.

Suddenly he turned, clutching her shoulders and forcing her to turn toward him. "Jessica. Listen to me. I was wrong to ask you to have an affair, no strings attached. I never should have done that. I know it. I knew it at the time, but I refused to face what I felt for you."

She finally allowed the tears that had been begging release to flow to their freedom. The darkness was overwhelming. She couldn't see his expression and was comforted in the fact that he couldn't see hers either. Her hand came up to make contact with his chest, only to slowly work up to cradle the side of his face, his chin, and jawline. His beard was slight, as if he had just shaved before going out, but it could still be felt.

"Does that mean you don't want me after all?" Her voice was husky, throaty in its timbre.

"My God, no! I want you more than I've ever wanted anything in my whole life." His lips came over to kiss the palm of her hand, his own hands straining against her back to bring her unresistingly closer to him. She rested her head against his chest, afraid to hear the words that would follow, not knowing what he was going to say.

"I don't understand. What do you want from me, Gar? Please, leave me some dignity to raise my own daughter. Please."

"Darling, I want you to marry me," he said,

and she was stunned. Her body stiffened before an overwhelming joy bubbled through her.

"Say that again."

"I want you to marry me. Now. Next week. I don't give a damn. I need you, Jessica."

Suddenly the bubbles popped, one by one, and she returned to the reality of their situation. She pulled her body away, but her hands were still reading his features in the dark. She was afraid to let go of him, but she knew she couldn't stay. Slowly, even though he couldn't see her, she shook her head no.

"It won't work yet, Gar. You aren't ready," she answered sadly.

"What the hell does that mean?"

"I mean you'd resent me in your home. You aren't ready to share the raising of Susanna. You aren't willing to have another woman in your home, and with our first argument, you would compare me to Carla. You'd see us both as the same woman and I'd lose you. I couldn't bear that."

"Susanna is ready for a mother. In fact she needs one. She needs and wants a sister and perhaps some little brothers." His voice was low, rumbling in the confines of the silent car. "But make no mistake, I want you for me and no other reason! And I couldn't begin to compare you to Carla. When she left me she left our daughter behind and and took our pet dog, a poodle. A poodle! Can you ever see yourself

181

leaving your child and taking a damn dog?" His bitterness was there still, but entwined with it was something she had never heard from him before—a realization of the humor of the situation. He could finally see the funny side.

"Oh, Gar, I love you so!" she murmured, plying his face with exuberant kisses. "Yes, yes, yes, yes, yes!"

His breath came out in a whoosh, as if he had been holding it in. "I was prepared to have you sit out here all night until you promised me you'd be mine. You gave me quite a start by telling me I could have you on my terms. I wasn't sure you knew what my terms were."

"I didn't care," she replied honestly. "I just knew I had to have you." Suddenly she remembered her date back at the restaurant. "Poor Arnie. I hope everything's going all right for him."

"Don't worry," Gar said with a dry tone. "He was promised a large order on his lumber if he could get you to that restaurant. He won't be hurting."

"You set this whole night up?"

Gar leaned over and flipped on the dash lights so he could see her. His face was tender in the dim light. His finger trailed down her cheek, following the path of a tear. "Yes, I set it up," he mocked softly. "I knew you weren't going to consider what I had to say until I had you alone."

"I see," she teased, her hand stroking his thigh and hip as she watched his immediate reaction to her touch through half-closed eyes.

His breath seemed to be caught in his throat as he watched her and realized she knew exactly what she was doing. "And do you agree on having another child?" his voice rasped softly in the quiet confines of the car.

"Several."

"And do you want them all conceived in cars?"

Her hand stopped. Her eyes opened wide. She saw his grin. "No way," she stated emphatically.

"Then it's a good thing you moved your hand. I'm certainly not a teenager anymore, but I'll be damned if I can refuse you for very long."

He slipped out of the car and waited as she slid out behind him. He snapped on the garage lights and opened the door leading through the utility room and into the kitchen. Before they even reached the second doorway, Gar swung her around and into his arms.

"My God, I love you, the future Mrs. Pace," he muttered, his mouth poised directly over hers without touching.

"And I love you. But I would love you more if you delivered what you promised and didn't keep a lady waiting," she whispered in return, her arms securely around his waist.

His lips came down to possess hers in tender passion. Moving slowly, they captured and held her prisoner as his tongue traveled the soft confines of her mouth, sending sparks of delicious sensations through her system. She arched toward him, feeling his instant response and reveling in it.

Giggles from the living room intruded on the silence and brought a groan from Gar.

"I thought they were staying at your house tonight?" he muttered under his breath.

"No, they're both here," she answered with a chuckle.

"In that case, we're going to your house." He turned her around and aimed her back toward the door, then stopped. "I need you, Jessica. I need to make love to you so desperately, but I don't want to rush you," he said very softly, his hands caressing her arms as he spoke.

A shiver went through her. "You're not rushing me, Gar. I need you too," she said honestly.

Without another word he hustled her out the door and toward the car. She gave an impish grin as he opened the door for her. "What would you have said if I said no?"

"I wouldn't have said anything. When all else fails, go to plan two."

"And plan two is?"

"Taking you home, kissing your sweet mouth, and massaging your luscious body until you'd claw tigers to get at me."

"I'm ready to claw tigers now, and you haven't even begun."

"Just wait, you witch. Just wait. I'm going to give you all that you deserve and more."

"Can you give me a pocket full of rainbows?" Her voice was light and airy, almost giggling, as she remembered Sheila telling her fortune.

"I promise I'll try, darling," he said earnestly. "I promise I'll try."

And he did.

Candlelight
Ecstasy Romances™

$1.95 each

Irving Wallace
The Almighty

Watch this man defy the world in his egomaniacal drive for power.

When the hunger for power becomes a craving, it's not enough for Edward Armstead to merely head a vast news empire First he must shape the news, then control it, and ultimately create it—even at the risk of global chaos. Only one person dares defy him: she's young and beautiful, and believes that no one should assume the awesome power of the Almighty.
10189-1-37
$3.95

For every woman who has longed to combine independence with devotion to family

Life Sentences
Elizabeth Forsythe Hailey

In *A Woman of Independent Means*, Elizabeth Forsythe Hailey wrote about a brave woman asserting her independence during an unliberated time. In LIFE SENTENCES she has created a different but equally dynamic heroine—a woman who acknowledges her *inter*dependence, who chooses love and commitment. It is unforgettable. $3.95